Mr Carrick
IS LAID TO REST

For G.

Mr Carrick
IS LAID TO REST

Inspector Wickfield Discovers Why

Julius Falconer

PNEUMA SPRINGS PUBLISHING UK

First Published in 2009 by:
Pneuma Springs Publishing

Pneuma Springs Publishing
A Subsidiary of Pneuma Springs Ltd.
7 Groveherst Road, Dartford Kent, DA1 5JD.
E: admin@pneumasprings.co.uk
W: www.pneumasprings.co.uk

A catalogue record for this book is available from the
British Library.

One

I must reassure you immediately that Mr Falconer is not ill – to my knowledge. He has not gone away, he is not in prison, he has not been kidnapped, he is not incapacitated, his typewriter still functions, his wits are (more or less) about him. My Friend, I am writing this to you today for the simple reason that he cannot be bothered. He tells me that he is tired and is therefore taking some rest. This, it seems to me, is a dismal state of affairs – particularly so in a man of his relative youth - but it leaves me free to tell you the story of a case that has been in my files for some years but which Mr Falconer has not yet, for reasons known only to himself, managed or contrived or perhaps summoned up the energy to squeeze into his schedule[1]. My name, by the way, is Wickfield, and I am a detective inspector with the Worcestershire force; but you may think of me simply as Stan, if you prefer. I therefore invite you to settle down and to accompany me, in your thoughts, into classroom 5b of Grant College for Girls, where our story begins in the year of grace 1974. The lesson, conducted by Mr Adrian Carrick, is one of philosophy for the Upper Sixth as part of preparation for an international qualification in the subject. We eavesdrop.

'Right, you horrible lot,' Mr Carrick is saying. 'Your essay is due in on Wednesday week. Remember, I want a beginning, a middle and an end - in that order: none of your post-modernist structures, thanks very much. That applies to you, Denise, in particular.'

---

[1] I have just been rereading this typescript to prepare it for Mr Falconer's perusal, and my conscience smites me. I cannot let the sentence pass without a further remark, because it does him – possibly! – a great injustice. If you have followed some of my other cases, whether penned by myself or by the affable Mr Falconer, you will know that you get Wickfield warts and all. Now in this case before us in the present volume, I commit one of the most egregious blunders in the annals of British policing – well, in my career at any rate (and it cost a girl her life): you will read about it soon enough if you persevere over the next chapters. (However, I am putting this admission into a footnote, in the slender hope that it will escape your attention.) Mr Falconer, I believe, may have left this case out of account – to spare my blushes! God bless him.

'That's not fair, Sir!' Mr Carrick chooses to ignore this interjection.

'You may discuss the subject among yourselves – in fact, I want you to - but the essay must be your own work.' A bell sounds in the corridor outside. 'Ah, nicely timed. That'll be all for today, then, folks. See you tomorrow: it's the lesson after lunch.'

The pupils depart. One remains. This is Geela[2], a dark, pretty thing, with hair tied back and a cheerful face.

'Mr C, have you got a minute?'

'Of course, Geela.'

'I just wanted a few more details about the bloke Descartes copied his ideas from.'

'I didn't say he copied ideas from anyone. I merely said that quite a few of the ideas that come up in Descartes are also present in a medieval Jewish philosopher called Maimonides. He talks about wax in heat, about humans being a combination of a conscious soul and an unconscious body, about how the senses mislead us, and so on.'

'How do you spell him?

'M-a-i-m-o-n-i-d-e-s, Moses. Lived in Spain. Died 1204 or thereabouts.'

'And the name of the book?'

'*Guide for the Perplexed*. It was originally written in Arabic, but it's been translated into English, more than once. Do you want to know which chapters as well? And page numbers? Look, you don't have to remember all this.'

'But I want to impress the examiner.'

'I know you do, but no examiner can expect you to remember masses and masses of such detail. Don't worry, you'll do all right. You've worked hard, you've got the brains. Relax.'

'Thanks. See you tomorrow, Mr C,' and Geela waltzes off to join her friends.

At this point, I may as well come clean: since the case had not yet come to my attention – did not in fact exist – I am fabricating these early pages! Before you close the book in disgust, may I explain? In

---

[2] I hope the inspector will not mind if I insert into his typescript at this point, by way of discreet footnote, a comment to the effect that the G in Geela is hard. I know this because I have looked it up! JF

the later stages of the case, after the second murder, I was obliged to reconstruct for myself, and for my sergeant, young Spooner, the situation out of which we thought the murders arose – well, they did and they did not: they arose from that situation, but not at all in the way we had at first imagined; that may sound confusing, but I cannot say anything more at this stage without confusing the story, and we cannot have that, can we? - and while there was no attempt to recall the precise words spoken or the precise gestures used, enough detail, including, as you will see, an impromptu reconstruction of a snatch of Plato's *Republic*, was furnished by the girls later on to build up a plausible picture of Adrian Carrick's philosophy lessons. I am simply trying to put you in the picture, so that you can accompany me, step by step, as the inquiry unfolds. Please bear with me, therefore, as I continue to set the scene and introduce you to some of the characters, notably Geela. It will become apparent where my lively imagination ends and where my notes, on my first introduction to the case, begin. Just allow yourself to be drawn into my, as ever chrysological, account of the case; I do not think you will be disappointed.

Adrian Carrick walked along to the staff-room for his mid-morning cup of tea. The staff-room was an unremarkable space, carpeted, with a scattering of easy chairs loosely arranged around individual coffee-tables. Along one side of the room stood a counter on which the necessities of simple refreshment were available. Opposite, a wall of windows looked out on to a non-descript yard where prefabricated classrooms had once stood but which now lay there, bleak and empty, a place solely for pupils in transit. Beyond, a strip of grass led to the junior school, housed in the old stable-block, and, to the right, a new sports centre could be seen. Carrick took a seat at random and found himself next to one of the French teachers.

'How's Geela doing for you?' he asked his neighbour.

'Geela? Oh, so-so. I'm not sure she works very hard. Difficult to say sometimes. She's got enough brains and savvy to get through without much effort. Why do you ask?'

'I've heard from German that she's not working very hard there either, and I'm a little concerned she won't get the grades she needs for uni. She's a nice girl, deserves to do well. She's doing fine in philosophy, but that on its own won't get her to Exeter. I'd like to see her a bit more galvanised, but most of it's out of my hands.'

'You mean Margaret and I should be doing more to get her moving? Well, perhaps she relates to male teachers better.'

'Oh, I get on with her all right, and she also seems to have the right sort of motivation in the subject. Well, we'll see. Not long to go now. Excuse me a minute, Joan, must catch Fiona before she slips away yet again.'

A few days pass. We return to classroom 5b, where a lesson is drawing to its close.

'Now can I just remind you – when Claire has finished inspecting her finger-nails – that tomorrow's lesson is a round table. I gave you all a copy of Book 1, chapter 19 of Montaigne's *Essays* last week, and if you haven't read it yet, you blooming well should have done. You've probably left it too late, and that'll ruin everything. Anybody not read it? You all have? Good. The topic for discussion is, Had Montaigne been reading the *Nicomachaean Ethics*? Shouldn't be beyond any of you – except perhaps Claire, who seems to have her mind on other things at the moment. OK, folks, that's it for today. Remember to bring the texts tomorrow – and your brains, of course: those of you who've got any to spare after your daily stint of mind-numbing pop music, dreaming of your boyfriends, writing letters to your admirers, watching TV and so forth.'

'Don't watch TV, Mr Carrick: too busy studying!'

This comment is naturally greeted with cries of 'Liar!', 'Suck!' and 'Rubbish!' The pupils depart.

'Yes, Geela. You're hovering.'

'Mr C, have you got Montaigne in the original; that one essay, I mean? Only it'll help me with my French. Kill two birds with one stone.'

'I have, actually. Here: page 63. You *are* keen, but I don't think you'll find it easy. Montaigne's French is quite tricky. By the way, now you mention French, how are you doing in it?'

'OK, I suppose. I keep up. I'll get a B, probably. I just can't stand Mrs Webb.'

'Yes, OK, but I can't sit here listening to you abusing other members of staff. See you tomorrow, then.'

'Bye, Mr C.'

One final glimpse into Mr Carrick's philosophy lessons, if you can bear it! I am including this scene because it illustrates perfectly, I believe, Mr Carrick's technique as a teacher at the higher levels of secondary school. You may judge its quality for yourselves. I gleaned the material at a 'philosophy workshop' with the girls concerned, much later on in our inquiry.

'Now next week, girls,' says Carrick, 'we must make a start on Popper, and I'm giving you now – don't lose them! – some notes on why Popper disagreed with Hume on the question of induction. By teasing out the problems in Hume's statement, Popper was led to a fuller formulation of his own theory of conjecture and refutation – which I'm sure you'll all find quite fascinating! Read through the notes, discuss them amongst yourselves – some hopes! - and then we can get cracking straightaway on Monday. Today we need to finish off Plato's *Republic*. Now if you remember, I asked Kirsty to prepare us a little something on the Simile of the Cave in a modern version. What have you come up with, Kirsty?'

'Well, Sir, I thought about it –'

'Yes, we take that for granted.'

'– and I came up with a little dialogue between myself and Jennifer.'

'Splendid: fire away!'

While Kirsty is tall and willowy, with long, blonde hair, Jennifer is quite a large young woman with brown hair in a boyish style. They present a somewhat comic aspect in their double act. To their credit, the girls had brought in a cardboard model to assist them in their presentation.

'I'm Socrates,' Kirsty says, 'and Jennifer is Glaucon, but because those aren't modern names, we're going to call ourselves Kirsty and Jennifer.' Some hilarity ensues. The two move to the front of the small class, take up a stance with their back to the blackboard and begin, reading from sheets.

K. 'Human life, you see, Jennifer, is like being in a cinema: we are so absorbed by what is going on on the screen that we forget that it's merely a reflection of real life, a shadow. Philosophers – that's us, Jennifer, members of the Carrick Academy for Well-Bred Young Ladies – see through the pretence and prefer real life to mere entertainment on a two-dimensional screen.'

J. 'Yes, I'm with you so far.'

K. 'Then you'll understand that once someone has realised the shadowy nature of what the average cinema-goer takes to be real, she will be reluctant to return to her first convictions.'

J. 'Yes, that's only to be expected.'

K. 'Now a further conclusion is possible – stay with me, Jennifer. The process of knowledge, of getting to know things – and we all want that for ourselves, don't we? – is a question not of acquiring new things but of directing our sight to what is already there.'

J. 'I'm with you all the way, Kirsty.'

K. 'Good. Now the philosopher is the one person capable of turning people round so that they face the projector and realise their mistake.'

J. 'Yes, I see that.'

K. 'But the people won't want to, will they? just too much trouble.'

J. 'So what's the answer, Kirsty?'

K. 'The answer is, we have to compel them.'

J. 'That's hardly fair, it seems to me.'

K. 'Maybe not, but remember that our legislation is designed not to favour any one class but to promote the welfare of the entire republic, and therefore those with knowledge must assist those without. That's only sensible. They won't wish to, of course, because they'd rather gather wool in the clouds –'

'Isn't that a bit of a mixed metaphor?' someone from the floor asks facetiously.

'– but then those who would like to would make unsuitable rulers, because their motives would be selfish and coarse.' There is more in similar vein. Kirsty turns to Mr Carrick and says, 'That's it, Sir. What do you think?'

School reception is, naturally, in the front hall just inside the main door. The visitor enters under a grandiose portico in Palladian style and is greeted by the view of a double, imposingly curved staircase leading to the first-floor grand central hall. The front hall is thickly carpeted. It contains a large bowl of cut flowers, a board displaying photographs of pupils engaged in school activities, and a large statue of the Sacred Heart of dubious aesthetic quality. The receptionist is speaking into the telephone.

'No, no, that's no trouble. I'll see you get that in today's post. Bye-bye, Mrs Grosvenor.' Replacing the receiver, the receptionist said to no one in particular, 'What a fusspot that woman is,' and then to her visitor, cordially, 'Yes, Adrian?'

'I'm expecting a small parcel. Anything come yet?'

'No, sorry. Unless Doreen's spirited it away. Is it important?'

'No, but I don't want it to get lost.'

A gaggle of sixth-formers enter the reception area, presumably to sign out.

'Hi, Geela, hi, girls. Where are you lot going, I wonder.'

'Only into the town – with permission – all above board, Mr C!'

'I didn't suggest it wasn't. Behave yourselves, remember – although looking like that, you could be mistaken for the inmates of a borstal.'

'What's a borstal?'

'Prison for young offenders. What do they teach you in current affairs these days? No, don't answer that, I don't want to know – at least, not just now.'

As the girls disappear, the receptionist chooses to express a view.

'Some of those girls aren't suitably dressed, in my opinion.'

'What? Oh, yes, girls will be girls. They're too young to know any better, most of them.'

'That Geela isn't, though. Mature, intelligent, well brought-up girl. Too pretty for her own good. I hope she knows what she's doing. Don't the form-teachers keep an eye on them?'

'Not my area of responsibility. Right, must be off, Gina. See you tomorrow – if the Lord spares us.'

'"If the Lord spares us": you're a gloomy one, and no mistake.'

Parents attend the last day of term in large numbers for the ceremonies that conclude the academic year, notably the prize-giving. On this occasion Mr and Mrs Purdew make a point of thanking Mr Carrick for his care of their daughter over the years. They meet on the expanse of lawn in front of the college, on part of which a marquee has been set up to provide strawberry teas. The grand sweep of lawn leads away from the front to a footbridge over a stream and thence, through a thicket of rhododendrons – and not just ponticums, either! – to tennis courts and hockey-pitches and woods where the pupils may walk. It is a proper summer's day, on which the stone lions couchant perched regally on the parapet on either side of the central pediment in the façade might feel at home.

'You know, Mr Carrick, you've done Geela a power of good,' says Mrs Purdew. 'She's really enjoyed these last two years' philosophy lessons, and they've given her an enthusiasm for matters of the mind she didn't really have before. You'll never know how much we owe you.'

'Well, thank you, Mrs Purdew,' is the modest rejoinder, 'but really the traffic has been the other way: it's been such a pleasure having Geela in the class, she's made all the difference. If only all our pupils had Geela's gifts!'

Mr Purdew is a senior inspector of schools and his wife a television executive: plenty of money, therefore, between them, but the upbringing of their only daughter has not suffered through undue indulgence of her. Two of Geela's friends approach the small group: Denise and Iona, looking their best in uniform for once smartly worn.

'We're sorry to interrupt,' says one, 'but Geela's having a bit of trouble with her shoes and wonders whether you, Mrs Purdew, could come over and lend a hand.'

After the departure of the girls and his wife, Mr Purdew comments to the teacher that one advantage of a school like Grant is the opportunity of meeting well-brought-up young women with personality and style. This comment, of course, exists only in my reconstruction (since, at the risk of repeating myself, I was not present), but I am quite sure it coheres with the parents' assessment of the school.

The term came to an end, as terms inevitably do. The senior pupils found themselves launched into a world of higher education – addresses of accommodation, even if it is only in halls, reading lists, details of courses, identity of tutors and the protocol incident in approaching them, a new batch of friends - or into the employment market. Some would retain their ties with the school; others would not. Some would return for landmark public functions; others would never darken the oaken doors again. For staff, there was the clearing up, new lists of pupils, new courses, adjustments to be made to old courses, a new timetable with which to come to psychological grips. Geela had left a note for her philosophy teacher.

Dear Mr C (he read)

I'm writing this to you instead of telling you face to face because if I tried, I know you wouldn't let me finish and you'd be far too modest.

I want to thank you for being the only truly inspirational teacher I have had in my school career. Philosophy this year as the only lesson that made me want to go to class! You didn't just teach to make us pass an exam, you made us rethink things we too easily take as certain. You managed to do the unthinkable and make teenagers enjoy a school hour!

Thank you for taking the effort to inspire us to debate, think and read even out of class. I have enjoyed so much learning from you and I hope that you've taken something from our many hours' debating: whether the sun will appear tomorrow, whether Plato's similes are bizarre or genius, whether we exist (a special favourite of mine) and the rest!

I will always remember the fallacies – they're just so useful. Thanks also for introducing me to Sartre, Camus, Kierkegaard & Heidegger (I may yet have to perfect the spelling). I have spent many a night debating with Iona about existentialism, me extolling its virtues and Iona preferring to stick with the objectivists in the teleology camp!

Learning about Kant on our philosophy road trip to Exeter was brilliant too, the speaker was really interesting. Despite the fact you wouldn't let us educate you about the wonders of modern music! I haven't had time to make you the mix CD but I will and I will write you a bit about each song explaining why I think the lyrics mean something. That will be my way to give you some new knowledge – no, it won't be dire!

Freud & Jung were wicked. It was good to be able to pick anything and learn about it without thinking I will have to know this in an exam! It was great to see where they agreed and clashed.

I'm not sure about Diogenes, possibly a bit mental, but who dictates what's normal? I like how he refused to suck up and lived by his own rules – the first existentialist?

Thank you, Mr C. Without you school would only have been a means to an end because of you I love thinking and learning. We never got round to Nieztsche (spelling?), but I've bought *Thus Spake Zarathustra*, and I really hope we'll be able to discuss it together! I'd really like to keep in touch if that's OK with you. Even if you don't hear from me for months – due to travel/work/whatever – don't think you've got rid of me! I may just be out doing the things that if I don't do them as I lie dying I'll wish I had done. And I've no intention of dying wondering.

Love and gratitude (for expanding my tiny mind!) always,

Geela

To this handsome letter, Mr Adrian Carrick penned the following reply:

Dear Geela

You say the nicest things! I may reciprocate by saying that when a teacher is faced with such an enthusiastic bunch as you lot, teaching too is a pleasure! You as an individual have worked hard this year and contributed much to the classes: you deserve to do well.

Yes, let us keep in touch. I shall follow your career with interest, and when you're world-famous I shall boast quietly to myself that, to however small a degree, I helped you on your way!

Look after yourself, Geela.

Yours ever

Adrian Carrick

PS Now you're of age, have left school, are a young woman etc please use my Christian name, if you feel you'd be comfortable with it. And no, it's not Muggins!

Other communications passed between them. May I give you an example?

Hi Mr C

I hope you get this note. I haven't time for more than a few words. So I am in situ at the château. I'll send you a postcard to show you what it's like. I'm OK, much happier now I have the car and can go out and do stuff with the kiddywinks we've been to the market today and I am planning to go out to the cinema soon! 6 weeks does seem a long time though and I do miss Pershore quite a lot but I do like to travel and see new places so …

The kids are sweet which is good the Duchess is very proper and I don't think she has warmed up yet, but hopefully that will change!

No, I think I'll stick with Mr C: not out of formality, but by way of affection. Thanks anyway.

Enjoy your weekend

Stay cool

keep in touch

lots of love

G

xxx

To this note, Mr Carrick replied as follows:

Dear Geela

Thanks for your note of a few days ago, with absolutely no information on your stay in France whatsoever! When I was exactly your age, in the year 18- (but we mustn't give my age away, so the nearest century will have to do), I toddled off to France to fill part of a gap-year before going on to university. I became *assistant d'anglais* at a Jesuit boys' school in Versailles. My duties (insofar as I can remember back that far) was to provide two hours of English conversation five days a week – not onerous – and for the rest I was entirely free to do as I pleased. I learnt two main things (I think): one, that Paris is an interesting city; two, that the proper way to speak French requires putting a light emphasis on the end of words and the end of sentences. By the time I left, my spoken French was much, much improved, even though we had had a very good teacher at school (up to A-level). I also got to know Versailles quite well. My outstanding memory is of weekly teas with M et Mme Renoir, who lived just down the road from the school. He was nephew of the painter Renoir, and she was a Cézanne, and I once counted fifty-two Renoirs and Cézannes dotted haphazard round their living-room! The rest of the house was full of books, room after room of them, piled high from floor to ceiling, over three storeys. A lovely couple.

However, *revenons à nos moutons*. Yes, let's meet before the autumn term starts, if at all possible. I have something particular to tell you, and something particular to ask you.

In the meantime, don't tell me anything about your duties, the household, the area, your feelings, your reaction to the French way of life: you might accidentally slip in some information.

Love

Mr C

Two

The telephone-call that follows is (again) my reconstruction, but I trust you will agree with me that it is a plausible effort: my fertile imagination has worked hard to produce a conversation that sounds authentic and matches the circumstances. I cannot enter the inner world of Adrian Carrick; but at least I have tried!

'Winslow, is that you? Adrian here. How's things?'

'Fine, thanks, just fine.'

'And Judith?'

'Yes, in rude health.'

'Good. Look, have you got a minute? There's a little matter I shouldn't mind mulling over with you.'

'Certainly. Go right ahead. You're not in trouble, are you?'

'No, no, not trouble, nothing like that. It's just that I can't get my thoughts straight, and a second mind might just help, even though it's yours. There's a girl at school – just left, actually – and I find myself physically attracted to her.'

'Well, that's not your fault, is it? One can't always help one's feelings.'

'No, I know one can't always help one's feelings. I'm not making a confession, just stating a fact. I don't feel *guilty* about being attracted to her.'

'And what does she think?'

'I've no idea, I haven't asked her, and I wouldn't ask her either. As far as I know, she hasn't the faintest idea that I am attracted to her in that way.'

'So what's the problem?'

'The problem? The problem is this. What do I do about it?'

'Tell her.'

'No, I can't do that. I don't think a direct, or even an indirect, request for intimacy would be moral. I simply can't do or say anything to initiate physical activity. Look, for heaven's sake, I'm sixty, she's a kid of eighteen: it just wouldn't be right. The alternative? I shall have to tell her frankly that I've screwed up the relationship – well, I haven't exactly, but my psyche, or my libido, or whatever it is, has screwed it up – and that I can never see her again. That's the only way we both ever going to be safe. Then I shan't be hanging on the end of a telephone, or sitting at my front-door waiting for the postman, or alternatively bombarding her with messages just to keep up the contact.'

'OK, do that, then.'

'Well, I'm not thinking just of the practicalities: the whole moral side disturbs me.'

'What moral side? You've just told me you don't feel guilty.'

'I don't, but you're not being very fair, Winslow. By "moral side" I mean what I do about it. I would do nothing to hurt this girl.'

'But we've just been through that. What's her name, by the way?'

'Geela. As I see it, there are three possible outcomes. I tell her what I feel and she spontaneously offers a physical relationship; I'm not sure I'd want that or be ready for it if she did, and in any case, if I can imagine that happening, my grasp of the female teenage psyche is probably even more fragile than I thought. Or secondly, I tell her what I feel, and before she has a chance to comment I announce that this is our last meeting and that all contact must cease forthwith. Or thirdly, she throws up her hands in horror and runs screaming from the meeting. So how will she react? That's all part of the problem: I haven't the faintest idea. I've taught girls for years without gaining any real insight into how their teenage minds work! There is another course of action, but it's not a feasible alternative: carry on as we are, me longing to possess her, and she oblivious of the true state of affairs. No, I couldn't stand that.'

'Look, Adrian, that's the front-door bell. Can I phone you back in a while?'

A little time passes before Adrian Carrick's telephone rings.

'Oh, Winslow, thanks for calling back.'

'Well, go on with what you were saying.'

'No, that's it: that's as far as my thinking has got.'

'And how urgent is a decision?'

'Well, I've got three weeks to carry on thinking. Geela tells me she's coming back to this country - she's helping out as an au pair in France at the moment - at the end of August and suggests we meet somewhere for coffee.'

'That sounds fine. You've got time to mature a reasoned and balanced decision.'

'Yes, I know that, but what I'm afraid of is that I shall lack the moral and spiritual strength to go through with it. Geela's the best thing that's happened to me for years – since Calandra died, in fact - in terms of lively and attractive female company, and I'm already saying goodbye after a few weeks!'

'Look, Adrian, why don't you just do what you think is best for her – be perfectly honourable - and then leave the rest to Providence?'

'You know, that might just be the most sensible thing you've said for ages. I'll think about that one. Thanks.'

However, there was a slight change of plan, as Adrian Carrick was to tell his brother in a telephone call a few days later.

'Winslow, it's me again, Adrian.'

'Yes, of course it's you: do you think I don't recognise your voice?'

'Look, everything's changed. Geela and I are meeting the day after tomorrow. Her plans have changed: she's been given a week off to return to the UK, for an early break, and she has written to fix up a meeting. This is catastrophic! Instead of having three weeks in which to think what to say and how to say it, I've got two days! I can't go through with it. I know I've got to: I committed myself earlier to speaking to her, knowing that I might get cold feet at the last minute. This is terrible!'

'Adrian, for heaven's sake, pull yourself together! You're a mature bloke of sixty. Be honest; be honourable! Consult her feelings, in so far as you can divine them. Then, whatever happens, your conscience will be clear.'

'OK, OK, I hear you. You're right, but this is a situation beyond my experience.'

Geela Purdew and Adrian Carrick met eventually at the Abbey

Tea Rooms in Broad Street, Pershore. I should perhaps just explain that Grant College was situated in its own extensive grounds outside the village of Bricklehampton south-east of Pershore. Adrian Carrick lived at Little Comberton, between the school and the town, while the Purdews lived in Pershore itself. This little corner of Worcestershire is in the centre of a triangle bounded by two railway lines and a busy A road, in the plain of the River Avon but within sniffing distance of Even Hill (app. 980 feet) – which is itself part of Bredon Hill - and possessing some of Worcestershire's finest countryside. Geela and Adrian met outside the Abbey, as arranged. It was a fine, warm day in early August. The stone-work of the parish church gleamed yellow and genial in the bright light. People were going about their business: shopping, sight-seeing, meeting friends, visiting professional enterprises, consulting their finances, or just loitering: it was a typical scene in a small English market-town.

'OK, Mr C, I nearly mistook you for a street-seller there! Where shall we go?' Ever the gentleman, as I hope my continuing reconstruction of events is impressing on you, Carrick said,

'No, I leave that to you.'

'OK, what about the Abbey Tea Rooms? That's civilised enough!' They walked into Broad Street – but why, oh why, do town planners allow such extensive parking on sensitive sites? – and entered the café, chose a seat in the window, ordered and began to talk.

'Right, Mr C,' said Geela, 'fire away. I'm intrigued to know what you have to tell me.'

'Let's eat a bit first. Relax, all in good time. We'll sink our gnashers into a scone first, if you don't mind.' This was to hide all sign of the state of his nerves. 'This is all on me, by the way.'

Inexorably the moment he dreaded approached: prevarication was no longer possible.

'Geela, I don't know how to begin.'

'Why not try the beginning: you were always telling us that!'

'Yes, but what is the beginning? Look, now the moment has come to speak to you, I'm too nervous to say anything! What I mean is, I don't think I can begin. Let's forget the whole thing.'

'You can't do that! You've led me on, I want to know what's on your mind.'

He paused uncertainly, torn between abandoning his project and blundering into speech.

20

'Right. This is precisely why I committed myself in a letter to speaking to you; because I knew when the moment came, I should try to back out of it. Here goes. Let me ask you to start with to keep this absolutely confidential. Don't tell Denise or Iona, or your parents. Please. But I also want to say that I am going to be honest with you, and I want you to be honest with me. The thing is, I hesitated to speak to you at all. Why should I share my problems with you? But then you are part – a major part – of the problem! I then thought that you're too young to be burdened with it; but you're a young woman; you could have been legally married for the last two years! You also strike me as being eminently sensible. In any case, I think people have, on the whole, a right to the truth. So here goes.'

'Mr C, you've said that already. Why not just get on with it, and I'll make of it what I can?'

'There's one other thing. I'm not expecting you to understand all I'm going to say: I don't understand it all myself. The thing is, I was expecting to have three weeks to rehearse what I was going to say and how to say it. Your unexpected trip back to England has left me just two days, and I haven't had time to get things straight in my mind. Your letter of Monday left me in turmoil, and I haven't sorted myself out.'

'Mr C!'

'OK. I'm beginning. Let's go back a year or two. I've known you from second year. Nothing remarkable there: nice girl, plenty of brains, quite a hard worker, at least in most areas, but I didn't notice you particularly. You won't mind my saying that, will you?'

'Mr C, get on with it!'

'Yes, right, get on with it. Then in First-Year Sixth, I got to know you very much better. In a smaller class, you stood out more. My affection for you grew. But there was nothing unusual in that. Then Upper Sixth: I got to know you even better. I realised you were my favourite in the class, but I didn't think there was anything strange in that; and I hope anyway that I didn't betray it in any way: bad pedagogical practice. Then just a week before the end of term – you probably won't even remember it – I met you unexpectedly at reception. I can't remember in detail what you were wearing – not uniform, anyway, and your chest was bulging out of the top of whatever it was you had on. I was taken aback, because it suddenly dawned on me: this girl is not just pretty, she's *desirable*, and that was

21

the moment it was borne in on me that I had been thinking of you physically for some time, without realising it. Since then, I have been in an agony of desire.' Geela opened her mouth as if to speak. 'No, don't interrupt. Let me finish. My first reaction was that I just had to keep this to myself. Apart from the fact that it would be quite inappropriate for a teacher to mention these things to a pupil, I was afraid you'd despise me and lose what I think is your good opinion of me.

'Can I now connect all this up with another couple of things that have been going on at the same time? I don't want to bore you, but I do want to try to make you understand.' Geela had fallen quiet – in her mind, I mean, as the weight of the situation began to dawn. I am trying to build up a picture for you of how I see things at that meeting.

'Please go on, Mr C: I'm listening.'

'The fourth anniversary of my wife's death is coming up, and I thought I'd just look through all the cards and letters that people sent me at the time. Many were from girls at the school or past pupils, and the thought struck me that all these nice people were vanishing into the past, were now strangers to me. I began to feel old and isolated. I had no achievements I could look back on, only a very lonely retirement to look forward to in a few years. That's one thing. I also realised that I hadn't had intercourse for five years, not since way before my wife died, because she had been ill for some time. Was the last act of intercourse in my life to be in my mid-fifties? So there's a lot going on in my head, to do with grieving for my wife, my personal identity as a man, my increasing age, and so on. I can't get it all sorted out. I have absolutely no stratagem for dealing with such violent emotions. And so we come to the nitty-gritty: what shall I do about it? what shall I do about you in particular?'

'Mr C, I'm sorry, but I can't take all this. I think I understand what you're saying; and I'm sorry for you. I'm sorry you lost your wife, that you're lonely, that retirement is weighing heavily on your mind. But there can't be any sort of future in our friendship if that's how things stand: can't you see that? There's really no sense in discussing it any further. It's just something you'll have to work through on your own. You haven't forfeited my good opinion of you, but I just feel uncomfortable with the whole business.' It was, however, as though she had not spoken.

'My first thought,' Carrick went on, 'was to ask that you and I never meet or correspond again. In my imagination we finished this conversation, then I asked you to give me a big hug and we parted – for ever; but I realised I just didn't have the courage or strength to go through with that. I then thought, well, let me give it ten years: ten years of silence, to see whether I can quieten my feelings, but I couldn't manage that either. Geela, would you agree to a year? Nothing from me. Can we then make contact again in a year?'

'I'm not sure that's a very good idea.'

'Look, I feel absolutely terrible about all this. I'm not aware of having done anything wrong, but I feel as if I'd let you down somehow. I enjoy your company very much: if only I could keep that level of relationship, without its tipping over into something much less desirable! OK, it's probably easier for you to get in touch with me, isn't it? I'm not going to move, whereas you could be all over the place, almost anywhere. That is, get in touch with me *if you want to*: you'd be under no obligation. How would that be?'

'No, I'm too confused to think. I'm sorry.'

'I'm sorry too. Perhaps I shouldn't have spoken at all; it just seemed right at the time.'

'Look, I'm going to say goodbye, I think that's probably best. Thanks very much for the tea, Mr C. Perhaps we shall meet again. In the meantime, look after yourself, and I hope you feel better about things eventually.'

With that, she rose briskly and made to leave. Carrick rose. They hugged briefly, and then she was gone.

The following day, Carrick wrote Geela a letter. Why she preserved it long enough to present to the court is unclear.

Dear Geela

I write this the day after our tea and scones together, to say thank you for proposing to meet me and to tell you that the meeting has made me far worse. You were tender, warm, sympathetic, a listener; in a word, womanly: everything that simply reinforced my regard for you. I have no stratagem for dealing with such violent feelings: I have tried long walks – two hours yesterday evening, four and a half hours this morning –

reading, prayer, the Bible; nothing works. I shall simply have to work through the matter over time, but because I have no experience of these things, I am unsure how long it might take or whether there not might be a shorter way.

When I got home after our meeting, I was in turmoil. Had I done right? had I said the right things? had I offended you? I went for a two-hour walk to try to clear the cerebral arrangements that in my case pass for a mind. Couldn't eat, couldn't sleep. So this morning, as I say, I went for a four-and-a-half-hour walk. No good. Except for one thing: I began to realise that my attitude to you was improving: less a fixation (with your physical person) than an obsession (with you as an individual). There may not sound much difference between these two, but to me the second is much more manageable. The cause of the change was your demeanour in the café: as I thought, tender, warm, sympathetic. This enabled me to take a broader view. Then the following day your letter arrived:

> 'Hi
>
> I thought about it more – I don't think even after a year it's a good idea for you to contact me. I don't want it to hang over me, I'm only 18 & that's too much for me to handle. Throw this away now – don't reply it wouldn't be a good idea. Just forget. Throw this away!!'

You're probably right, but it's desperately hard to take. I'm so confused I no longer know what I want, but I think I could lay my inner turbulence to rest if one last word from you assured me of your forgiveness and that you will not spend the rest of your life repelled by your memory of me. I may have done you wrong, but it was done with the very best of motives: to spare you the attentions of an elderly admirer, for ten years: well, at least a year, until I could get my regard for you on a more even keel. That would give me hope that I could continue to enjoy news of your career and life.

This is the last you will hear from me, but you will be ever in my thoughts. God bless you, Geela.

Love

Adrian Carrick.

Four days later he was dead.

Three

Before I proceed to tell you how I came to be concerned in this affair, let me sketch in what I learnt about Adrian Carrick. First of all, the man. Physically, he was of slight build, tall, with brown hair and green eyes; far from handsome but not unpleasant to look at; ordinary, really. In character, he was complex. An obvious feature was integrity, in two principal directions: he was honest in facing up to his own weaknesses and foibles, a man without self-deceit and without self-delusion; and he was sincere in his attempts to follow his conscience, treating others as he would wish to be treated himself, with respect and openness and acceptance. He did not merely *follow* his conscience: he *cultivated* it, so that it was informed and living and constantly maturing. This trait might, in some, have led to self-possession and poise, but in Adrian Carrick it led to self-doubt and a lack of confidence, so that people noticed in him a curious shyness for one who spent most of his professional life as a teacher. Intellectually, he was well-favoured, some might even say clever, except that his gifts were spread too thinly for him ever to make a massive contribution in one area. By that I mean that his interests were wide and diverse, enabling him to draw in scholarly nutrition from a large number of stimuli: music and history, poetry and other literature, languages, philosophy, architecture, anthropology, cosmology and natural history, and this gave his teaching breadth and vigour, but there was never time to develop any one of these in depth.

What else can I tell you about him? He disliked people who gossiped, people whose conversation did not rise above the trivial, people whose conversation consisted entirely of personal anecdotes. These were so many further reasons for his avoidance of society. He despised the triviality of the age in which he lived. He found relief from the world's troubles and hope for their solution in religion and prayer. He had prejudices but worked valiantly against them, preferring to base his life and motives on reasoned judgement and religious sentiment. He supported a dozen charities and worked as a Samaritan. I could go on. He was, I get the impression, an honourable and worthy individual. You will appreciate that, since I never met the man in life, I am concocting this portrait of him from information received!

Then to the details of his life. He was born in 1914, of middle-class parents, in Salisbury, where his father worked at the cathedral as Keeper of the Fabric. At the age of sixteen he won an open scholarship to Oxford, attended Balliol College for three heady years, graduating three years later in PPE, and then, through one or two contacts, set himself up as a freelance translator of philosophical texts, mainly for London publishers. Two considerations persuaded him to abandon this path: working at home made for a quiet social life – not that he was a socialiser, but there was a limit to the amount of eremitism compatible with the hunt for a wife!; and it did not pay very well. (He was paid by the thousand English words of the completed translation; but one had to add on to that the time taken to type the work up, draw up an index – and that consumed vast amounts of time on its own and required considerable skill - check the references if literature referred to was available in English, read the proofs and undertake the other editorial services required if the final work was to be fully presentable.) Reluctantly, therefore, Adrian Carrick cast around for alternative employment and hit on the idea of teaching. With this in mind, he suffered the year's lectures that went by the name of a post-graduate certificate of education at a red-brick university in the northern provinces before applying for and eventually obtaining a post as a teacher of Spanish and philosophy at a school near Exeter (such a glorious cathedral!). In time he concluded his teaching career as a member of staff at Grant College for Girls. On the way he had married and, as the reader knows already, been widowed, and had a son and a daughter, at the time of the events of this narrative away from home, married and themselves parents.

We have already touched on the interests that occupied his lively mind. In his spare time he gardened, played the piano, walked extensively, wood-worked and collected stamps. He was above all a *serious* person, in the sense that he willingly bore the responsibilities incumbent on someone in his position, with an eye to his duties towards the society in which he lived.

How was Adrian Carrick rated by his employers? His head-teachers, over a teaching career spanning something over thirty years, seem to have regarded him favourably. He was assiduous in his lesson-preparation and marking and in the other duties incident on the life of a secondary-school teacher; he got on well with the pupils, particularly, perhaps, the less able ones, whom he patiently encouraged; he contributed to school life outside the classroom. However, his daughter told me that he always doubted his effectiveness as a teacher and would have abandoned teaching if he could have seen his way to any other career. He was forever comparing his performance in the classroom with that of other teachers whom he admired and suffering from the comparison. To be tormented by uncertainties of this nature is grave in a professional person; it saps one's self-esteem, sometimes to the point of suicide.

My problem was to work out why someone would wish to kill this seemingly harmless, upright and worthy citizen. Since in the end – as will, I hope, become clear – our suspicions surrounded Geela Purdew and her circle, I must also tell you something about Geela. I came to know her quite well, partly because there was the advantage in her case that she was alive. Of winsome appearance, she struck me as being a confident and articulate young woman, with a ready laugh, a sympathetic manner and the ability to attract and be the centre of a group of friends without ostentation or affectation. I have already had occasion to mention her intellectual competence and her personal warmth. I make only two reservations, neither of them (I suppose) very weighty. One was that I deplored her taste in pop music, which favoured what I think is referred to by some as grunge – nihilistic, anarchic rubbish about as mindless as you will find anywhere on the planet – and her lack of industry in some areas of her academic life. I wished to be clear in my mind about the relationship between Carrick and Geela. Had she led him on? The answer I came up with, after talking to her parents, friends and teachers, was, Definitely not. She was not sufficiently sophisticated; or, to put that in more positive terms, she was too nice a person. Geela was seemingly not provocative or forward: just an ordinary teenager with personality, good looks and intelligence on her side.

'But wither am I going? I had almost lost myself.' I apologise that I find myself having to quote the, however entertaining, Izaak Walton. Although Carrick lived in a cottage that stood on its own to the north of Little Comberton, just off Wick Road, a milkman called every other day with a pint. Several days after Carrick's last meeting with Geela in Pershore, the milkman noticed – how could he not? – that his previous delivery still stood on Carrick's doorstep. He knocked but received no answer. He peered in at the windows but could distinguish nothing unusual. At the conclusion of his rounds, he thought he would mention that matter to the local constabulary, and he was assured that it would be investigated. It was investigated. The constable appointed to carry out this task, PC Yvonne Richardson, found the house in order but empty. On the desk in a corner of the sitting-room was a sheet of typing paper carrying what appeared to be the first sentences of a diary-entry (except that it was not in a diary). This is what she (and I later) read:

> I must and do respect Geela's wishes in the matter; she has no choice but to consult her own heart, which, heaven knows, is warm and open. For my part, however, the conflicting emotions in my head know no diminution; I am torn hither and thither in the most disturbing manner. I must be strong. I must recognise the emotions for what they are: the manifestations of a lower nature, unredeemed, unwanted and treacherous. *Sois sage, ô ma douleur, et tiens-toi tranquille.* Only poets as seamy as Baudelaire speak to me in my anguish. So, what next? I must work through this, with patience and fortitude, and emerge victorious the other side. This is not a basis for self-destruction, and yet

Here the handwriting, firm enough to all appearances, broke off. Alarmed by her reading, PC Richardson suggested to her superiors a search of the locality. Since Carrick was known not to possess a car, and since his bicycle was safely lodged in an outhouse, the police safely deduced that he had left the house on foot. Tracker dogs led the search-party over a track from Little Comberton to the slopes of Even Hill, along to the northern summit, by the so-called Banbury Stone, and then into the woods below St Catherine's Well, where an old quarry rested after its labours. At the bottom of the quarry lay the inanimate remains of Adrian Carrick.

There was, naturally, an inquest, held at the court in Stourport. The account of it with which I furnish you here is second-hand, since I was not involved at that stage, but it will not lack interest or style for that! The coroner, Mr Terry Hackett, was a brisk and efficient officer of the law. Initial witnesses testified to the identity of the deceased (the son and daughter), to the discovery of the empty house and the circumstances that led to its search (PC Richardson), and to the discovery of the body (Sergeant Fleming). Allow me to give you one extract from this latter exchange.

'Sergeant Fleming, could you just tell the court what arrangements are in place to secure the quarry from unwary walkers?'

'Well, that is to say, Sir, there is a fence, some ten yards from the lip all the way round: a wire fence strung between concrete posts. However, over the years, people who have wanted to peer into the depths, as you might say, have broken sections down, so that the quarry is effectively open to the path in parts.'

'And is this damage of long standing?'

'Yes, I should certainly say so, Sir.'

'Does this suggest that the local council has been negligent in its duty to protect the public?'

'No, I'm not saying that, Sir, it's not really my place to comment. The quarry is not really a danger to anyone, as the fence posts make it quite clear where the path ends and the lip of the quarry begins. That said, repairs to the fence might not be a bad idea.'

The next witness was the headmistress of Grant College, Mrs Glenda Howard, who, having been sworn in and taken through her statement, deposed as follows.

'The police naturally approached me, as Mr Carrick's employer, and asked whether I could shed any light on the fragment of writing that the deceased was apparently working on at his death. Geela is an unusual name, and I had no difficulty whatever in recognising under that designation one of our recent leavers: a prefect, a sports captain, a pupil of whom we have high hopes. I can confirm that Mr Carrick numbered Geela amongst his philosophy pupils. I have made inquiries amongst the staff and senior pupils close to Geela, and all testify that there was never the slightest suggestion of impropriety in their relationship. Mr Carrick never exhibited the least favouritism in her regard, and he maintained with her the same respectful and correct relationship as with all his pupils. There was no suspicion whatever of anything improper. May I say that Mr Carrick's death has come as a great shock to us? He was a much valued member of the community, and we are grieved to think that he may have come to harm in connection with his work with us.'

It was inevitable that the next witness to be called was Geela herself. She was soberly but fetchingly dressed, with the bloom of youth on her cheeks and a serene if sombre look in her eye. When I tell you that the attention of the whole court was on her, you must understand that that is not a mere statement of physical fact. The press saw to it that the inquest was a matter of intense local interest. The coroner, basing himself on her previously submitted written statement, plied her with questions (addressing her always as Miss Purdew), so that matters might be made quite clear to the court, and this was the gist of her testimony.

'I knew Mr Carrick from my first days at the school, because I took Spanish as one of my subjects. I regarded him as a good teacher. When, therefore, the time came for me to choose my subjects in the Lower-Sixth, I had no hesitation in putting down philosophy as one of my options. The course was taxing but very stimulating. Mr Carrick would break up lessons with cryptic crossword clues, to teach us lateral thinking, or "round tables" to develop our expository and debating skills, or little pieces of practical philosophy to illustrate the relevance of the subject to everyday life. We had one particularly lively debate on whether the sun or a million-mile-wide bowl of tulips would appear over the horizon in the morning, and what rational grounds we had for believing the former. We as a group all knew each other well, and we got on fine. No, I could not say that he showed me any partiality; he was always perfectly proper. When I left school, at the beginning of July, we met for a coffee in town – I can't remember now who initiated this – a week after the end of term, just before I was due to go off to France to take up a three-month placement as an au pair. We got on fine – a perfectly respectable and reasonable conversation. I had a letter from him, a few weeks later, saying he had something to tell me and something to ask me next time we met, and I was, of course, slightly intrigued but certainly not apprehensive in any way. Originally I was not expecting to return to the UK before the end of August, six weeks into my contract, but my employer changed her plans and asked me whether I should mind taking my week's break a little earlier than arranged. I wrote to Mr Carrick, giving him details of my new movements and offering a new date for a meeting. He agreed, and we met. It was only then that he unburdened himself.

He told me that he had physical feelings towards me, that he regretted these, and he hoped I should agree not to meet or correspond again for twelve months. That was more or less it. We embraced on parting, because that was the normal thing to do, but I came away in a turmoil of emotion. Thinking things over later that day, I wrote, or rather scribbled, him a note, which I posted there and then, saying that I thought it was better we never met again.'

I conclude my summary of her testimony with an exchange between the coroner and her.

'You say in your statement, Miss Purdew, that Mr Carrick mentioned an occasion, or perhaps I should say the occasion, on which it dawned on him that he was physically attracted to you. This apparently took place in the reception area of your school, when you were not in school uniform. Do you have any recollection of this?'

'No, not in the slightest. I don't remember anything about it: not what I was wearing, or where we were going, or being seen by Mr Carrick.'

'So you cannot be precise on how long he had had feelings for you?'

'He never hinted at any such feelings until our meeting which ended our relationship.'

'Your meeting with him on –' consulting his notes – '6 August was, therefore, if I understand you correctly, your first and only intimation that he felt warmly towards you, in a physical way?'

'Yes, it was.'

'Would you say that you encouraged him in any way in the generation of such feelings?'

'No, no, certainly not. The very idea would be abhorrent to me.'

'Had you any inkling of the depth of emotion he was experiencing?'

'No, how could I?'

'Did his final letter to you, which you have quite responsibly agreed could be shown to this court, give you any idea that he might be so disturbed as to contemplate suicide?'

'No, not at all. I knew him to be a religious, serious sort of man, with plenty of inner resources. We all have moments or phases of intense emotion, and I certainly never had reason to believe in his case that he would not manage to overcome this – crisis, if, indeed, it was a crisis.'

'Miss Purdew, I must reassure you that the purpose of this court is to find out how, and if possible when, Mr Carrick died. Apportioning blame is quite irrelevant, so I hope you realise that I'm not in any way suggesting that you had a hand in Mr Carrick's state of mind. You seem to have acted throughout, if I may say so, with extreme good sense and as a young lady should. Nothing we have heard in court implies that you have anything at all for which to reproach yourself. I trust I make myself quite clear. Nobody is blaming you in the slightest.'

The coroner called one more witness, Geela's best friend Denise. Miss Denise Phethean was similar in build to her friend but a little thinner – admirers might have called her lithe – a straw-coloured blond, with sharper features and a crooked tooth, but poised and articulate. She testified that Adrian Carrick had never given signs of favouritism, to Geela or to anyone else, that his demeanour was always appropriate, both in and outside the classroom. His feelings for Geela had come as a complete surprise to her.

'I understood from Miss Purdew's statement that Mr Carrick asked her to divulge nothing of the conversation she had had with him in Pershore. Have I been misled?'

'No, Geela – that is, Miss Purdew - told me that Mr Carrick had asked her not to disclose to any else what he was going to say, but she felt justified, in the confusion of her feelings, to confide in someone. There's surely nothing wrong with that?'

'No, no, Miss Phethean, I'm just trying to clarify Mr Carrick's state of mind. Miss Purdew has told us that he assured her he was not ashamed of his feelings, but I was wondering in that case why he should wish to keep them secret. If his conscience didn't trouble him, why should he be so concerned as to wish to take his own life?'

'With respect, Sir, it wasn't the bare fact of having feelings for Geela that troubled him, as I read the matter: it was rather whether he had dealt fairly with Geela in his disclosure of them. He would never have wished to cause her pain.' She paused.

'You may continue if you wish,' the coroner said, kindly enough, 'providing that what you say is relevant.'

'Mr Carrick once told us that in his view friendship was so valuable it needed to be treasured and cherished and worked at. He used to quote – did he say it was from Pope?[3] - "Cultivate thy Friends/Friendship life grace lends". My understanding from what I know and from what I've heard in court today is that he was grieved for the loss of a friendship when Geela said goodbye. He wasn't ashamed: he was sad, and he blamed himself for the break.'

The coroner's summing-up, as it appeared in the official record of the proceedings, and in the light of the evidence and of what the police investigation later turned up, was, I thought, fair. 'Ladies and gentlemen,' he said, 'the case before us has presented regrettable aspects but is not, I believe, peculiarly difficult. A teacher, by all accounts an admirable one, is taken unawares by the potency of an emotion that is for him unusual, and he finds it difficult to cope. He makes no advances towards the object of his aspiration: on the contrary, he retreats, and that can only be set down to his credit. Now a person ill-disposed towards Miss Purdew might argue that, by denying Mr Carrick the hope of a meeting in twelve months' time, she drove him to suicide. No right-minded person would go along with this. It is not this court's business to lay blame, but even if it were, no accusation can sensibly be laid at Miss Purdew's door, on this head or on any other: she has, in my view, acted entirely properly throughout. No, the emotions which persuaded Mr Carrick to write the letter and the note which this court has seen were the product of his own psychic processes, and my belief is that they proved too powerful for him. On his own account, he tried various remedies to extricate himself from their coils, and these included long walks. On one of these walks, but less than three miles from his home, he found himself at a spot which was, I daresay, very familiar to him, and to which access was easy. The possibility of a fatal leap must have presented itself to him in his anguish, and although the quarry is not deep, the rough surface at its bed would have caused instant death. I therefore bring in a verdict of suicide while the balance of the deceased's mind was disturbed.'

That was that: no mystery, certainly nothing that would warrant any action on the part of the police; another misfortune in the long annals of human misery, soon to be consigned to the dustbin of memory - until that is, a man walked into Pershore police station nine days after the deliberations of the coroner's court.

---
[3] I do not think this is Pope. JF

'Good morning, Officer,' he said to the constable at the desk. 'My name is George Bolster, and I live at Little Comberton. I am a near-neighbour of Adrian Carrick's.' He was a man of about sixty, with a lugubrious face and a twitchy hand.

'Yes, Sir,' the constable said encouragingly.

'I have just returned from a fortnight's holiday abroad, and I read the account of the inquest into Adrian's death.'

'Yes, Sir.'

'I have a piece of information that might be useful.'

'Right-ho, Sir, let's just organise a piece of paper and a pen, and we can make a proper job of it. What is the information you desire to impart?'

'On the day of Adrian's death, I was walking my dog on Even Hill, making for Ashton under Hill, you understand, where I intended to have a spot of lunch at The Star. They do a lovely ploughman's, Officer, as you may well know: fresh bread, great hunks of English cheese, the most gorgeous pickled onions, and the beer is really moreish. It was a warm and cloudless day, but because it was a weekday, there weren't that many people around.'

'Am I meant to be writing all this down, Sir?'

'No, no, I'm getting there; give me time, Officer. Anyway, there I was, just coming to the top of the rise, with Morley – that's my spaniel, you know – well, a bit of a cross really, but to the casual eye he would pass as a spaniel - romping about and loving it, when I saw two men ahead of me walking at a slightly oblique angle to the direction of my own walk. They disappeared into the trees to my right, and I carried straight on.'

'Yes, Sir, I've got all that. May I ask why you wish to report this?'

'Well, don't you see, Officer, one of the men was Adrian Carrick!' Since no expansion on this remark followed, the constable prompted him.

'And who was the other?'

'Oh, I've no idea, but Adrian was quite unmistakable, even from the back.'

'And what time would this be, Sir?'

'Well, Officer, I've tried to calculate that as best as I can. You see, I set out from home at ten o'clock – in the morning, of course. You're

34

not imagining this took place at night, I hope? Now normally I should expect to get to the top of the rise within half an hour, but I stopped on the way to chat to old Mrs Warburton – such bad legs, you've never seen anything like them – and then I lost Morley in the woods, where he'd gone off chasing a rabbit, I suppose – so let's say it was about ten minutes to eleven when I saw the two men.'

'Can you describe the other man, Sir?'

'Only very vaguely, I'm afraid: rather squat and broad, sleeveless top, some sort of sunhat, a cream thing with a brim all the way round, and trousers.'

'Trousers?'

'Yes, well, what I mean is, he was wearing long trousers, whereas Adrian was in shorts.'

'Ah, I see, Sir. Would you recognise him again?'

'No, not a chance. They were not very close, I saw only the sides of them briefly, and Adrian hid the other man from me, and then their backs for a short while – a very short while, but I certainly didn't recognise him from the back.'

'And what is your reading of what you saw, Mr – er, Bolster?'

'Well, don't you see, Officer, if I've got my facts right, Adrian Carrick was in the company of another man minutes before he went to his death!'

Four

When the DCI called me into his office to hand me responsibility for the case, he was sympathetic.

'Look here, Wickfield,' he said, 'this may be a wild-goose-chase. What you're starting with is the very slenderest thread, and it may lead precisely nowhere – even if you manage to grasp it to start with. Now you and I haven't always seen eye to eye, but on the whole I have full confidence in you. That's why I am entrusting this case to you. Do your best, but I shan't blame you if you make nothing of it. Understood?'

I knew this to be a load of flannel, saving your presence, but I do not think he realised that I was fully aware of this. DCI Maxwell gave me the case because, knowing that success was unlikely, he would not risk the reputation of his pet officers. There I was, then, landed with a case in which the entire evidence, if that is what it was, was a vague sighting of an unknown man. Full stop. Not much, I think you will agree. Pity me in my predicament. Of course, Wickfield was up to the challenge, as I shall now proceed, with becoming modesty, to tell you.

When I summoned Detective Sergeant Spooner to my office to share with him our new instructions, he must have noticed a glum look in the corners of my eyes.

'What's up, Sir? Not like you to be downcast.'

'Well, thank you, Sergeant. You are particularly perspicacious today. Am I normally a ray of sunshine, then? Perhaps I am, but today we have been handed a poisoned chalice – or do I mean an apple of discord? or perhaps even a hot potato? Anyway, the long and the short of it is that a schoolteacher called Carrick was found two and a bit weeks ago at the bottom of a quarry not far from Bredon. The coroner brought in a verdict of suicide, but our DCI wonders whether it might not have been murder. He has therefore summoned his favourite investigative team and given us the thankless task of looking into it. He knows full well that our chances of success are as near zero as makes no difference, but he doesn't think another failure on our score-sheet will be noticed. Nice of him, I must say. Actually, he never said that. Forget it: the remark is a by-product of my bitterness.'

'What's given him the idea that the coroner was wrong?'

'As I understand it, the coroner was not wrong: he brought in the only possible verdict on the evidence available. What has given our DCI other ideas is a sighting of a second man with Carrick just minutes before Carrick leapt or fell to his death. That's what we've got to follow up.'

We had perforce to begin with Mr George Bolster, our dutiful informant: there was no other possible starting-point. We called on him that afternoon, at his cottage in Little Comberton, one of the older houses in the village.

'My goodness, Gentlemen,' he said, 'that was quick! I spoke to a constable only this morning. You're lucky to find me in, actually, as I was just about to go out to stretch my legs.'

'We shan't keep you a few minutes, Sir,' I assured him. 'You made a clear statement this morning, and all we wish to do is to go over it with you – just to check we've got it straight and to ask whether you might not be able to expand it.'

When we were sitting in his front room, I began by thanking him, on behalf of the force, for his selfless devotion to his civic duties and by assuring him that we considered his testimony invaluable.

'Would you start from the beginning and tell us everything you saw?'

'Right, Inspector. Today is Monday. I got back from holiday on Saturday – Torquay: lovely beach. Met some pretty women, too, but I daresay you don't wish to hear about all that! Anyway, I was catching up on some of the papers yesterday and read for the first time about Adrian Carrick's sad death and the coroner's verdict.'

'You knew him then, Sir? How well, would you say?'

'Reasonably well, I think. We used often to chat in the street and occasionally went for walks together. Nice bloke. Unassuming. And he didn't talk all the time, as some folks do.' He said this without a trace of irony. 'Anyway, on that Saturday – the 10th: I checked the dates carefully, as I didn't want to make a fool of myself at the station – I was up on Even Hill walking Morely –' the dog's ears twitched momentarily – 'when I saw Adrian ahead of me.'

'About how far away would you say, Sir?'

'Don't know: fifty yards, maybe? Anyway, he was with another man, and they were walking at a fairly brisk pace.'

'And you couldn't be mistaken?'

'No, Inspector, I couldn't. I'd recognise Adrian at twice that distance. The two walked on but rapidly disappeared to my right into the woods below St Catherine's Well. By the time I reached the tip of the woods, they'd long since disappeared.'

'Did the dog react at all?'

'Oh, yes, he picked up Adrian's trail, all right, but I soon whistled him on, because we were heading in the opposite direction.'

'And can you describe this other man?'

'Well, only what I told the constable this morning. You see, I just didn't get a good enough look at him, and in any case they were in view only for a matter of five or six seconds. How was I to know identification would be important? There was Adrian out walking with a friend: so what? I had no reason to take particular notice, had I?'

'Did you get any impression of how they stood to each other? You used the word "friend": did the way they walked suggest friendship to you? Adrian wasn't being forced in one direction, was he?'

'No, I shouldn't say so. They looked, well, normal: how any two people look when they're walking together.'

It was all very unsatisfactory: beyond a couple of bare facts, we had nothing. We therefore thanked Mr Bolster for his time, and we took our leave.

The village of Little Comberton, with its essentially twelfth-century church, St Peter's, at the southern end, and its old cottages and rural setting, is a peaceful and picturesque settlement and an unlikely setting for murder – or for a murder plot, perhaps we should say. We decided to ask around a bit, knocking on doors on the basis that someone may have seen a stranger, or Carrick in company, or

38

someone calling at Carrick's cottage, or a car, and we struck lucky. If we had not, our investigation might have come to a halt as soon as it had begun. It so happened that the morning of Carrick's death, the paper-boy, who was indisposed (so his mother said), had not turned up for work, and the newsagent himself had to deliver the papers later in the morning. When he called at Carrick's house to deliver his newspaper, he noticed standing outside it a new car. I asked him why he should notice it. Well, said the newsagent, it was parked right across the front gate: no problem for Carrick himself using the back door, but awkward for someone wishing to post anything through the letter-box at the front. Why did he notice it was new? Because it was the first N registration he had seen. Then, as he squeezed past, the newsagent continued, he read the supplier's name in the back window: Horsfield's of Worcester. Horsfield was his wife's maiden name. That is why it made an impression. What kind of car was it? A Volkswagen Golf, he thought. Colour? Dark green – he thought. Excellent, I told myself! Here was something to go on at last! I was jubilant: although of course if I had taken a moment to look up and scan the peak we had yet to climb, I should have been more moderate in my enthusiasm.

We drove off, in our – my! – elated state, to Horsfield's of Worcester, asked to see the manager and explained the nature of our business. Horsfield's had sold three green Golfs in the first ten days of that month, with the new registration number. Of course, Murphy's Law applied, and the first two buyers we approached had irreproachable alibis and seemingly nothing to hide. On the other hand, I suppose I should be grateful that the bulk of British citizenship seems to be law-abiding and civilised. Our third buyer was a Peter Symons, of 27, Foxwell Street, in the Upper Battenhall area of the city, and here we were luckier. We caught up with Mr Symons as he returned from work that afternoon and were immediately discouraged to see that he did not in either detail match the vague description furnished by Mr Bolster: he was neither 'squat' nor 'broad' but, on the contrary, tall and, if the truth be told, rather weedy. More promising, however, was the look of guilt that spread over his bony face when we introduced ourselves.

'If it's a parking fine, Officers, I'll pay up at once.'

'No, nothing like that, Sir. May we come in?'

The house was a terraced property close to the railway, well looked-after, with a pleasantly fresh smell. I asked him where he had been on Saturday 10 August.

'Ah, that was my first free day after I'd bought the car – you see, I knew you'd called about the car - and the missus and I decided to take her for a spin.'

'And where did you go, Sir?'

'To the seaside, Officer: south coast.'

'Would you like to tell us in that case how it was that your car was seen outside a house near Pershore?'

'Was it? Ah. It wasn't involved in a crash, though; and you said there was no parking offence. So what was it?'

'What about telling us the truth, Mr Symons? Much better that way.'

'Well, you see, Officer, it was like this, only I don't think you're going to believe me.'

'Try us.'

'Perhaps we should sit down?'

We sat in his living-room. We had not mentioned the business which brought us to his house, but already he had volunteered a parking-fine and a false story. We waited.

'On the Friday night, I was in the pub with a couple of guys, and I told them I had just bought a new Golf. One of them said he'd thought of buying one himself and wouldn't mind a look over mine some time. The other one said, 'I'll go one better: let me drive it tomorrow, and I'll give you a hundred quid.''

'What, just like that?'

'Well, more or less. He said his own car was in for major repairs and he had an urgent job on. We fixed up details: he was to pick the car up outside my house at eight o'clock in the morning and drop it back before five, leaving an envelope in the glove compartment.'

'And you trusted him?'

'Well, I knew him – sort of, that is, by sight, and the other bloke was a witness. I didn't think there'd be any harm in it. And a hundred quid's a hundred quid. In these hard times, you've got to pick up what you can, you know.'

40

'So what happened?'

'Well, that's what happened. He took the car, dropped it back, and that's all I know.'

'And where do we get hold of this gentleman?'

'I don't know where he lives,' Symons said hopelessly, with his arms outstretched. 'I know him only as "Danny", and I only ever see him in the pub.'

'And did you see his licence?'

'I took it for granted he had one.'

'Was he insured to drive your car?'

'No, I don't suppose so.'

'Why didn't he hire a car?'

'I didn't ask him.'

'Well, I'll tell you why, My Friend: he'd have had to show his licence, and there'd have been a record of the hire. This man wanted nothing on paper.'

Symons looked at us bleakly. I explained that we were engaged on a murder inquiry and that we had reason to believe that his car was used in the course of the crime. A uniformed officer would arrive in due course to take a full statement from him.

Our visit to Mr Symons was discouraging. It meant more inquiries. We finally caught up with Danny that evening in the pub, and believe it or not, he too shuffled off final responsibility.

'Look, Officer,' he said, as we stood in a corner of the pub as far from the muzak as we could get. 'There's this bloke I know. Bumped into him on the Friday afternoon. He said there was fifty quid in it for me if I could get him a reliable car for the Saturday, no questions asked. I was to drop the car off, with the keys in the ignition, at half-past eight precisely, outside the Horn and Trumpet in Angel Street, and I could pick it up again there at four o'clock. He gave me £150 there and then, and that was it.'

'Why on earth would he trust you with £150?'

'Look, Officer, you don't double-cross that sort; you don't let them down, either. I know better than to try anything on. In any case, it was money for old rope, so I went along with it.'

'Right, so who is he?'

'You've got to believe me when I tell you I don't know! Honest. I've seen him around, but I'd never spoken to him before.'

'It seems to me that all the crooks in Worcester know each other by sight but never know each other's names! Right, down to the station with us, and we'll look at a few mug shots.'

'Look, Officer, my life wouldn't be worth a tin of sardines if he thought I'd shopped him to the police.'

'We'll take care of that. We can't have you obstructing the police in the course of a serious investigation, so you'll have to come with us, no two ways about it.'

I am glad to be able to report to you that we achieved a modest success. We showed our friend Danny a rogues' gallery – the grim, the dour, the forbidding, the surly, the sullen and the morose – and from amongst them, with understandable hesitancy, he laid a finger on the photograph of someone well-known to us who went by the *nom-de-guerre* of 'Tomahawk' but whose real name was Johnnie Levers. Johnnie Levers, from a broken home somewhere in the Midlands, began a life of crime while still in his teens, graduated from the petty to the serious, and became eventually an assassin who could be hired for a modest fee. At the time of the death of Adrian Carrick, he was in his late thirties. He had been in and out of gaol numerous times, but he had never gone down, as far as I am aware, for murder. Levers was stocky and broad in the shoulders, a muscle-man with the brains of a sea-urchin, but none the less dangerous for that. Our investigation came to an abrupt halt at this stage, because when uniform went in to arrest him, the bird had flown. We supposed that someone had seen us talking with Danny in the public house and had tipped Tomahawk off. It was only a matter of time before Levers surfaced again, not necessarily on our patch but somewhere within easy grasp of the long arm of the law. Until, then, however, we were stymied. I had a conference with my sergeant.

'Well, young Spooner, what do you think?'

'We're not out of the woods yet, Sir, even at this early stage. I mean, how are we ever going to prove that Levers is the man Bolster saw? He won't have left fingerprints in Symons' car, and we haven't yet found anyone else who saw him with Carrick. Bolster's sighting wouldn't stand up for half-a-minute to cross-examination. We have, on the other hand, made a valuable gain.'

'And that is?'

'Well, as I see it, Sir, we can be fairly sure Carrick was put out of the way by a hired assassin. We can't prove Levers' involvement in this affair – not in a way that would stand up in court – but I'd say we were on the right lines. The question now is, who hired him? When Levers is caught, we can ask him outright, although the chances of his telling us anything are zilch.'

'Right,' I said, 'so I guess that our next step is to visit Mr Carrick's cottage and see whether anything there has a secret to reveal to us. Why should anyone wish to eliminate a harmless schoolteacher?'

Carrick's cottage was a mid-eighteenth-century property (I estimated) that had been extended in the twentieth century. It was rather attractive. Climbing roses up the front were still in bloom. The front-door led into a beamed living-room which ran the full width of the double-fronted house. At the back was a modern kitchen – in the extension – and upstairs were two bedrooms (above the sitting-room) and a bathroom and a study or small third bedroom (above the kitchen), with further stairs up from one of the bedrooms to a loft or attic which ran the full width of the house. A reasonable sized garden surrounded the property on three sides. A wooden name-plate to the left of the front-door proclaimed to the world – or that small part of it that was likely to venture up a lane in a small Worcestershire village - that the house was called The Cottage. There were a lot of books and bundles of papers everywhere, but the study seemed to be the likeliest place to contain any papers that might be of interest to us. Let me tell you, Gentle Reader, although I am not sure you will credit this, that we spent the whole of that Tuesday afternoon and the following Wednesday morning sifting painstakingly through wads and wads of papers, newspaper cuttings, old correspondence, notes, jottings, files of one sort and another, note-books, and envelopes stuffed with papers. Every time we had finished with a section, we had to put it somewhere where the other would not peruse it again and so waste our time, and we had to make sure that we covered everything that was there. How Mr Carrick could find his way around I am not sure, but presumably teachers have their methods, and he would probably claim that he could lay his hands without trouble on anything you cared to mention. The result of our search was nothing. There was not a single piece of paper that suggested to either of us that Carrick was the object of a contract on his life. We were baffled.

However, I realised then that there was several other avenues we had not considered: Carrick's son and daughter and his brother. They might just be aware of something that could put us on the right track. The brother, we discovered, had not long gone abroad on holiday: we should have to catch up with him later. Carrick's daughter, Frances, lived in Hereford, where she and her husband, Geoffrey, ran a small book-binding business. We called on the Wednesday afternoon, at their business premises in the town, and Frances Haslehurst said she would be happy to talk to us. She was in her mid-thirties (I should say), with long, unruly ginger-red hair, freckles and the most engaging broad smile. We had retired to an office where the noise of the presses was least audible.

'Mrs Haslehurst, may we start by assuring you that you have our deepest sympathy? Your father's death must have been a great shock to you. Were you aware that we are now treating it as a case of murder?'

'Yes. Someone at the police station was kind enough to inform us that an investigation had been put in place, although we were warned not to expect too much.' Yes, well, thank you for that, whoever you were. 'How can I help?'

'I want you to think back and identify for us, if you can, any sort of incident or trouble which might have a bearing on your father's death.'

'Look, Inspector, I've been thinking hard ever since your kind policeman telephoned us this morning, but absolutely nothing comes to mind. I've asked myself a dozen – fifty dozen – times, why anyone should wish to murder Dad. I was told that a short, burly man was seen with him minutes before his death, but that description means absolutely nothing to me.'

'Well, I can tell you, Mrs Haslehurst, that we now think he was a hired killer and so would be quite unknown to your father or to the family.'

'I see. Have you any idea what I should be thinking of?'

'Had anyone made threats, to your knowledge, or had your father ever mentioned in your hearing, that there was someone out there wanting revenge, wanting to pay off old scores? Had your father ever had dealings with gangs: drugs, high-performance cars, money-laundering, black market, people-trafficking (heaven help us!), art theft? - you name it.' I was probably sounding pretty desperate! 'Had he ever killed anyone in a car accident, been responsible for sending anyone to prison, brought about someone's financial ruin, pinched someone's wife – sorry! – anything at all? At the moment we're as much in the dark as you seem to be.'

'Look, Inspector, I'd love to help: of course I should, but I've cudgelled my brains to no avail. I shall keep thinking, of course, and I'll get back to you if anything should occur to me. In the meantime, why don't you have a word with my brother? He might just remember something.'

Five

Frances Haslehurst's brother Maurice lived in Birmingham with his wife and two young children. By profession he was an art-dealer: he ran a gallery in the city centre, buying and selling, attending auctions and viewings, holding expositions. Now I should be the last person to cast even the slightest aspersion on the world of art-dealers in principle, as, although my knowledge of art may be limited, I gladly acknowledge the huge contribution that art makes to the advance of civilisation. It is, in a sense, the key to understanding humankind's development as an intelligent being: it embodies his gropings towards an understanding, both individual and social, of his world. Writers have acknowledged its ability, on the one hand, to tell the truth:

It is the glory and good of Art

That Art remains the one way possible

Of speaking truth,

as Browning, for example, asserted, and, on the other, its ability to hide and disguise: Jonson talks about its 'adulteries', I seem to remember, and someone, perhaps Goldsmith – or was it Swift? - scorns the 'gloss' it so ably puts on things. In the matter of externalising the human mind, it takes precedence over music, sculpture, literature, architecture, theatre and dance. However – you guessed that there was a 'however', had you not? – art *dealing*, given the high prices paid for certain works, the fluctuations of the market, the desire of people to invest in commodities that do not just maintain but increase their value, and the ease with which paintings may be forged, altered and tampered with, has always risked flirting with the shady and the doubtful. However honest the particular dealer, there is always someone ready to come along and propose a deal: something to his or her advantage, wink, wink, nudge, nudge, say no more.

Spooner and I entered MC Galleries in New Street, Birmingham, with an open mind. Maurice Carrick summoned an assistant from the

46

depths of a storeroom to 'mind the shop' so that we could talk undisturbed in his office.

'Ah, Gentlemen,' he said, 'I was expecting a visit from you before long, as soon as I was informed that you had started a murder hunt.'

'And I suppose your informant also told you that there is only the very slightest chance of success?'

'He did.' I knew it: have I got 'Mr Blunders' tattooed on my forehead and have never noticed? 'I'm not sure I see how I can help.'

'Well, Sir, we should like to put to you the same question that we put earlier this afternoon to your sister: have you any reason to believe that your father had fallen foul of any criminal enterprise? You see, we now think that your father was the victim of a hired killer, which suggests professionals.'

'Inspector, you put me in a very difficult position.'

'Why is that, Sir?'

'Because I can't see the point of raking up sordid matters when nothing will bring my father back.'

'"Sordid matters"? So you do know something?'

'Very little, and I have done my best to forget what little there is. You are now asking me to produce it in broad daylight.'

'I am, Sir. This is a murder investigation, and society needs to know that the truth is told: the who, the why and the wherefore. Otherwise crime goes unpunished, and you can understand that that is not, *cannot* be, our policy.'

'I repeat, this can do no good. My father's reputation stood high, in the circle of his friends and acquaintances. That he lost his head over a pretty girl at the end is not to be set against him. What you now wish me to do is to sully his reputation beyond repair.'

'I'm sorry, Sir, at the moment you're talking in riddles. Wouldn't the best thing to do be to tell us what you know, and then we can take it from there if we need to? You can be assured that we are not going to make more waves than is necessary.'

'Oh, very well, Inspector, but it's little enough I know, as I said. About three years ago a letter arrived here, posted in Venice and written in Italian, and naturally I opened it. It was a reminder about abiding by the terms of an agreement of an art cartel: that's what I gathered, anyway. The word *cartello* was a bit of a give-away! I was stunned: I knew nothing about any cartel: complete news to me. I then looked at the envelope: it was addressed not to Mr M Carrick but to Mr A Carrick, and I had opened it by mistake. It dawned on me that my father was meddling in the art market. He was, I knew, reasonably knowledgeable in art matters, particularly, I think, in Italian art, but to get involved in a cartel – that was too much. Quite why the letter should have been sent to him here I'm not sure: an understandable confusion, I suppose, as I am probably the only Carrick in the book under art-dealers.'

'So what did you do about it, Sir?'

Nothing, precisely nothing, Inspector. I suppose I should have tackled my father about it, remonstrated with him, pointed out the folly of his ways, all that sort of thing, but two things dissuaded me.'

'And they were?'

'Firstly, it was his business. He was old enough to manage his own affairs, and he would have resented any interference from me. Secondly, I was, I admit, rather ashamed. I thought that if I did nothing, it would go away. Stupid, I know, but I was quite busy here at the time, and it seemed easier to ignore the whole matter.'

'Have you any idea how long they had been going on for: your father's dealings in the art market, I mean?'

'No, none at all. After that first letter, one or two others arrived – well, two, I think – with a Venice postmark, and I simply threw them in the bin. There hasn't been another for two years now.'

'Can you remember anything about them?'

'Well, the first one was typed, unsigned, and, as I said, in Italian. Something about Domenico this, Jacopo that - minor, well, relatively minor, painters of what the Italians call the Rinascenza, as I recall.'

'The Renaissance, as we say.'

'Well, not exactly: the early part of the Renaissance. The later part of the Renaissance, say from about 1530 to the end of the century, the Italians call the *Rinascimento*, but that's a detail. Such labels are only a convenience. There's one other thing I should perhaps tell you, Inspector. Since my mother died, Father has taken to popping over to Venice several times a year, so his art dealings may stretch back three or four years now.'

'Does your sister know about this?'

'No, I haven't told a soul, not even my wife.'

48

'And whereabouts in Venice did he go, do you know?'

'No, I don't, but the only address mentioned in the first letter was Hotel Le Streghe on the Lista di Spagna, apparently the venue for a rendez-vous. I don't know Venice very well, but if memory serves me the Lista di Spagna is the name of one of the main streets from the railway station down to the Rialto.'

'How on earth did you remember the name of the hotel?'

'Well, I remember saying to myself at the time, it's a bit odd naming a hotel after witches: doesn't *streghe* mean witches in Italian? Unless, of course, Paganini had stayed there.'

Having thanked Carrick junior for his assistance, Spooner and I returned to Worcester. On our way, I remarked that one thing I had noticed in Carrick senior's cottage which did not cohere with what we had just learned was an absence of books on Italian art, which was surprising in one who apparently wheeled and dealt in the subject. To be any good, you would need reference books, specific studies in various painters, auction catalogues, that sort of thing; yet I could remember none at The Cottage apart from general volumes which could be on the shelves of anyone aspiring to a general culture. We should have to check, as our search of Carrick's premises had not really encompassed all the stacks of books, but it set me thinking that perhaps the Venice address was a cover for something a little more elaborate than a hotel room. I began to smell a trip to *La Serenissima*, which, in late August, might not be too disagreeable!

DCI Maxwell was sympathetic: he felt sorry for me, I suppose. With so little to go on, I was clutching at straws, as he realised, and yet he could not allow the chase to be abandoned so early on in its progress if he was to justify an investigation into Carrick's death at all. On Tuesday 27 August, therefore, leaving the DCI to request permission from the Italian police, I flew out to Venice and booked into the Hotel Le Streghe for an initial two-day visit. What can I say about Venice, Dear Reader, that has not been said before? If you know the city, no words from me can embellish your memories. If you do not know it, no words of mine can convey an adequate picture. I carried my bag from the railway station the short distance to the hotel and immediately, even before ordering a coffee at the bar in the street outside, asked to be guided towards the police station, the *questura* --- England expects every man to do his duty. The Venetian authorities, alerted by DCI Maxwell to my visit, were putting no obstacle in my way. On the contrary, they assured me of their ready assistance if it should be required. *Grazie, signori!* Back at the hotel, armed with a piece of paper officially stamped, I begged a quiet word with the manager, and I was shown into a comfortable office on the ground floor inhabited by a dapper little Italian with a Poirot moustache. I explained the object of my visit.

'Yes, yes, *Signor Ispettore*, I know Mr Carrick. He has been coming for some years.'

'Do you mean he stays here? rents a room?'

'No, he does not. I mean that he collects his post from us.'

I told him that *il Signor* Carrick was dead and briefly outlined the circumstances of his murder.

'*Giusto cielo*: that it should come to this!'

He went on to explain that Mr Carrick used the hotel as an accommodation address, in exchange for a small fee. He popped in daily to check for post and telephone calls and then disappeared.

'And where did he disappear to?' I asked.

'Ah, that is a more delicate matter! You see,' the manager continued in a subdued tone, even though nobody could be eavesdropping, 'he clearly did not wish anyone to know where he lodged. *È meglio non correre rischi inutili*, or as you say in your bitter and chaotic language, discretion is the better part of valour. We respected his privacy, of course, but one day – I freely confess this, *Signor Ispettore*, because you are evidently a man to be trusted – I followed him, as I was anxious to know what we were harbouring. So I can tell you – privately – that he had a room in a *palazzo* just behind us, on the Fondamenta Venier. Very discreet!'

He jotted the address down for me and politely ushered me on my way. Here was a turn-up for the books! As we suspected, Carrick was leading a double life. In Pershore-land he was a humble schoolteacher plying his profession in the quietest way possible. Here in Venice he had secondary accommodation which placed him at the heart of international art dealing. I made my way to the address so cautiously provided by the hotel manager with the Poirot moustache and hunted up the *portiere* or caretaker or whatever his precise role was. Showing him my official accreditation and rustling a couple of 1000 lire notes in an inviting manner, I persuaded him to allow me entry into Carrick's apartment, where I stood alone to contemplate my target's double life. As I suspected, an entire wall was devoted to bookshelves on which stood, in serried ranks, books on painters and painting in every conceivable size and colour: mostly Italian, from what I could tell just by looking at the spines, but many also on French, Dutch and Spanish art, English portrait-painting, Russian iconography and some on cubism, impressionism and surrealism – an impressive spread of interest. Empty picture-frames stood in one corner, a dozen pictures were stacked in another. Most surprising of all, however – but then this demonstrates just how scanty my knowledge of friend Carrick still was – there was clearly a female on the premises: not physically, you understand, but in principle. The main bedroom, which was spacious and gracious, contained a double bed, and the wardrobe a range of women's clothes. There were, further, photographs round the flat of a glitzy woman whom I took to be Italian (she was not Chinese or African, but I suppose she could have been Portuguese or Finnish or perhaps Lithuanian – such were my idle speculations as I looked around me). There were no signs of recent habitation. On the contrary, there was stale food in the fridge, and some cut flowers in a vase in the sitting-room had withered for lack of watering. Still, I was clearly hot on the scent. It would have been useful to meet Carrick's lady-friend – and I yet might – but at least I had unfettered access to his correspondence and private papers.

I suspended my feelings of anticipation. We already knew that Carrick was the victim of a contract killing and that the killing was a punishment for some infraction of somebody's rules. I was about to flesh out the second life of Adrian Carrick towards which Maurice had pointed me, with its exotic setting, its attractive female helpmeet, its evidence of money in the making. What help would it be to identify the person or persons who ordered his elimination? He or they were doubtless members of an international cartel or gang who would be replaced as soon as one of them was tried and imprisoned. None of it would save Carrick now, and most of it would bring hurt to his family and friends. Then I condemned myself for my pusillanimity and defeatism. *All* crime was to be brought to book, within the limits imposed by police resources, because it weakened society and damaged mostly the poor. Then again, policing society was like offering a National Health Service: there would never be sufficient funds to treat every ailment and every patient; difficult choices of rationing and allocation had to be made – the work of hardened health-care managers, or, in the case of the police, of practised chief constables. Perhaps the death of an ordinary schoolteacher in rural England did not merit the allocation of one the force's senior, most experienced and most consistently successful officers. (I refer to myself, Dear Reader, in case the allusion had escaped you.) There was also the consideration that policing, like education and health, was a political football round which the various parties circled with an eye not to the common good but to electoral success, which was not at all the same thing, and I could not allow my own political beliefs to prejudice the conduct of the case. On the other hand again, I had been told to pursue the murderer of Adrian Carrick, and the decision had therefore been taken out of my hands. I therefore set briskly to work to unravel the secret of Carrick's double life.

I shall spare you a recital of the hours I spent riffling through papers of various kinds and extensive correspondence stretching back three or four years. Several times I tottered back down to the Lista di Spagna to refresh the inner man with an *espresso* and a *toast*, but by the end of the day I had built up a coherent picture of what Carrick had got himself into. In fact, if I understood correctly, Carrick was one of the leading lights and co-founders of the cartel, aided and abetted, during his absences particularly, by the lovely Faustina Scaglia (I had been right first time, if her name were any indication). The cartel specialised in early Renaissance Venetian painters and haunted the auction-rooms of Europe. A close eye on catalogues and other sources of information ensured that they knew when any such paintings were being offered for sale. Because they never bid against each other, they depressed the market, so that such paintings sold for much less than they would have done. After a year or two of that, acquiring works at a low figure, by bidding high they raised the price of such art and so made substantial profits. It seemed also, if I was correct in my appraisal of Carrick's papers, that the cartel were instrumental in introducing fakes from time to time, to ginger up or otherwise shape the market, working hand in hand with experts who either manufactured near-copies from scratch or who made genuine fifteenth-century paintings appear to be by the hand of masters rather than, say, of pupils. I also discovered that the glamorous Faustina, although no longer in the first flush of Mediterranean youth, made it her business - with what methods I hesitated to guess - to influence private collectors and the custodians of public collections in particular directions. It was, seemingly, a well-run if risky enterprise. Carrick's partner in business was a Swiss citizen called Ueli Fehrmann, who lived in St.Gallen. To St.Gallen I should need to go.

The following morning, therefore, I caught a train over the Alps (well, through the Alps) to Zürich and thence to St.Gallen. If you have never seen the *Stiftsbibliothek* in that city, you have missed an eye-watering rococo concoction that (to mix my metaphors) is jaw-dropping; but in a sense the entire city is of a piece with it. Anyhow, I digress. Mr Fehrmann was at home, the personification of suave conmanship, if I am any judge. He occupied an expensive flat in the centre of the city, with views through a picture-window towards the splendid *Kathedrale*. My host was cordial but also, I thought, wary. He offered me refreshment, and we sat on either side of a heavy, marble-topped, occasional table that would grace any room. I showed him my credentials, by this time endorsed by the Swiss authorities, and proceeded to ask him about his partnership with Adrian Carrick.

'Adrian? Yes, a nice man.' Mr Fehrmann spoke precise English with a slight, but only slight, German accent. 'We met a few years ago in Venice, where we were both holidaying. We had wandered independently into the Galleria dell'Accademia to view the collections, we got talking, as visitors do, and it became apparent that we both shared an enthusiasm for Venetian art of the Renaissance. We sauntered off for a cup of coffee together, and he proposed that we collaborated in starting up a house that specialised in such art. We discussed the matter at length, sounding possible backers, investigating the legal aspects of owning and running a gallery in Venice, when both of us were foreigners, looking at present provision in the city, and so forth, and the result was that we set up a small gallery in the Calle Selle, which we have run ever since.'

'Has it been successful, Mr Fehrmann, if you don't mind my asking?'

'It has, I am glad to say, although there have been troughs as well as peaks.'

'You will have guessed that I am here to inquire into Mr Carrick's murder.'

'Murder? *Du lieber Himmel!* You do not mean to say, Inspector …?'

'I'm afraid I do, Sir: on the 10th of this month, in England.'

'Well, well, I am stunned, I have to say. I had no idea. Honestly, no idea at all. There can be no mistake, I suppose?'

'No, none, I'm afraid. Of course, I didn't see the body myself, as I was brought into the case only later, but it was identified by his family, and there was a proper inquest. So I am here to ask you what light you can shed on the matter.'

'I, Inspector? None whatever, I can assure you. I am shocked. May I ask why you think I may be able to help?'

'Well, Sir, not to put too fine a point on it, we believe that you and Carrick were operating a cartel, that he fell out with you, perhaps by threatening to go to the authorities, perhaps by double-crossing you in some way, and that you ordered his death.'

'Inspector, this is outrageous. You have no right to level such accusations. There is not a shred of truth in what you say!'

'What can you tell me about *la Signora* Faustina Scaglia?'

'Oh, her! Not my cup of tea; much too garish for my taste. It was Adrian who invited her into the business, and I admit that she has worked constructively for us, but I confess that I do not care for her very much.'

'How had he met her, do you know?'

'I cannot help you there, I am afraid. I have as little to do with her as possible, although, as I say, she has proved very useful.'

'When I searched Carrick's flat in Venice yesterday -' Fehrmann's eyebrows rose significantly – 'I found evidence of a cartel and also of forgery. Would you like to explain that, Mr Fehrmann?'

'You are asking me to speak ill of my partner, Inspector, and I am loath to do so, but seeing that he is dead … I have sometimes feared that dear Adrian had ideas above his station. By that I mean that I sometimes thought running a small gallery in a Venetian back-street did not always satisfy his ambitions, his - shall I say, to borrow our neighbours' phrase - *folie de grandeur*. I had no idea, however, that he had created for himself a whole fantasy cartel, with fakery thrown in for good measure! *Menschenskind!* That also is news to me, I beg you to believe me.'

'You will forgive my commenting, I hope, Sir, but this apartment must be expensive to maintain. Does your gallery – as you describe it, a small gallery in a Venetian back-street – allow you to live in such style?'

'Inspector, I have two other galleries, one in Zürich and one in Paris, and between them my business interests allow me to adopt a life-style which suits me. There is nothing wrong with that, I hope?'

Six

As I travelled back to Venice, thinking that the fascinating Faustina perhaps held the key to Carrick's murder, I went over the three possibilities in my head. Firstly, Fehrmann was lying to me when he protested ignorance of Carrick's descent into crime. Secondly, the cartel was a creature of Carrick's imagination, summoned to enhance a lonely and uneventful life as a schoolteacher but lacking reality. Or thirdly, the cartel was real and had taken its revenge. I realised that I simply lacked the data on which to work. The correspondence I had seen in his Venice flat looked real enough to me, but it is not difficult to fake correspondence. On the other hand a real cartel, operated without his partner's cognisance, would have put him in an invidious position and possibly placed his life at risk in the sordid world of international art-crime. I was impatient to catch up with *la Signora* (*Signorina*?) Scaglia.

My train halted at Mestre. I waited a short time for a connection into Venice, alighted at St.Lucia and made straight for Calle Selle to see Carrick's gallery for myself. The Calle Selle was not exactly a back street, although clearly not as frequented as the Lista di Spagna, of which it was an offshoot. The frontage was elegant if not commanding, and the interior matched. My entry was the signal for a young woman to emerge from the shadows and bid me good morning. She was not Faustina, unless some very extensive plastic surgery had transformed her beyond recognition, but she was a pleasant and attractive young woman. We spoke in Italian until, after a few sentences, my accent betrayed me, and she lapsed laughingly into perfect English. Her laughter very quickly disappeared, however, when I produced my credentials.

'We cannot talk here,' she said with some urgency. 'We shall be better in the office.' Since the glazed door of the office commanded a view of the 'shop', it seemed not a bad idea.

'I am frightened, Inspector,' she said cautiously. 'Ever since news of Mr Carrick's death in England came through, everything's gone haywire. I presume that is what you've called about?'

'Yes,' I replied, 'and I am anxious to interview Faustina Scaglia as soon as possible. Can you tell me where she is?'

The assistant looked more apprehensive than ever and dropped her voice to a frightened whisper.

'No, I daren't,' she said softly. 'She's gone to ground, fearful that she will be targeted next.'

'Look,' I said, 'this is ridiculous. First of all, tell me your name.'

'Orlandina.'

'Right, Orlandina. I am hunting for Mr Carrick's killer. Faustina can tell me where things in the business have gone wrong and therefore put me on the right track. You have to tell me where I can find her.'

The conversation went to and fro, fear and tight-lipped lack of communication on the one hand, urgent insistence on the other. Eventually, by persuading her that it was in everybody's interest that the killer was identified and caught, I prevailed on her to give me a place of rendez-vous in Bologna, where Faustina, contacted by Orlandina on the telephone in the meantime, would meet me late that evening if she felt it was safe to do so. Cloak-and-dagger this undoubtedly was, but I felt I had no choice.

Now I do not take particularly to Bologna: a very handsome historic centre, with a quite splendid cathedral, but not much else. On the other hand, that could be said of half the world's cities. Not knowing how long my business in Bologna might take, I booked in at a hotel in the city centre. My rendez-vous was (as it transpired) in a squalid little bar in a side street off the Via Renato Torreggiani in the south-eastern suburb of San Lazzaro di Savena, in a neighbourhood in which I felt uncomfortable as daylight faded. I had been told to sit at a table inside, with a folded *Messagero* and a cup of coffee on the table, and simply wait. I waited. Faustina eventually appeared out of the garish gloom of the street and sat down beside me, swathed in a scarf although it was almost intolerably hot.

'We will talk in English,' she said. 'There is no chance of our conversation being understood,' she added, glancing furtively round her. 'Adrian Carrick's death in England is a sign that all our lives are in danger. I fear you will be powerless to help.' She spoke very good English but with an attractive accent.

'Look,' I said in exasperation, 'I can't help anybody at the moment because I simply don't know what's going on. That's why I've insisted on talking to you.' I then took a few minutes to outline what we had discovered about the circumstances of Carrick's death. 'Perhaps you'd like to start at the beginning,' I continued, 'and tell me all you know – and I mean all – about Carrick's enterprise here in Venice.' I rose and fetched her an *espresso* and a glass of *vino rosso* from the counter. 'Take your time,' I cautioned. 'I need to get the story straight. From the beginning.'

The evening was hot, but cooler than the day had been, and the suburban citizens of Bologna were strolling about arm in arm, or chatting in small groups, or doing a spot of late-night shopping. I witnessed this busyness from my vantage-point in the bar, but my concentration was focussed on the woman beside me.

'Adrian's Italian is very good,' she began. 'In fact on a good day he could be mistaken for a Piedmontese. He'd long harboured a yearning to run a place of his own, and when the chance came up to purchase the lease of a small, and rather run-down, art gallery in Venice he jumped at it. It would give him the chance to put down proper roots in Italy by establishing a long-term enterprise in a city he'd always loved. Because the flat above the gallery was not available, he was forced to look elsewhere and was lucky enough to hit on a flat in a *palazzo* just behind. I should perhaps tell you at this point that he had at this time met a Swiss art-dealer who was keen to invest in a place in Venice. The venture became a reality. Adrian asked me to be shop-keeper, so to speak, and soon found, I believe, that he could rely on me implicitly. He therefore allowed me to appoint Orlandina to take my place as shop-keeper, while I was free to focus on the more important jobs like meeting clients, whether buyers or sellers, attending auctions and expositions, and generally keeping an eye on the market.

'Because the business was going OK and making money, Adrian left it all to me so that he could engage in – well, shall I say, riskier enterprises. He had always been fascinated by the ease with which forgeries could be passed off as the real thing to gullible collectors.

58

Another way of skewing the art market was to operate a cartel. In both areas, a skilful operator who keeps his head can make a lot of money as well as enjoy himself enormously: it gives a sense of power, which Adrian enjoyed. Of course, all that side of his activities he kept to himself: it was safer that way, even though he could trust my absolute discretion. It suited me admirably, because I wasn't a bit interested in all that: I was quite happy supervising Orlandina in the shop and running the wider enterprise – Galleria Assunta - on my own. I was determined to make it a player on the international scene in the narrow window of style chosen by Adrian and Fehrmann.

'Now I don't know what went wrong or why. I have supposed that Adrian overreached himself. The areas of activity he had chosen to make his own were full of pitfalls, even for the wary. Perhaps he took his eye off the ball. Perhaps his rivals were more ruthless, or better clued-up, or simply more numerous. As I say, I knew virtually nothing of that side of things. Anyway, he told me that things had blown up in his face and that he was going to "retire" for a bit until the situation quietened down a bit. Then this,' she added pitifully, spreading out her arms in a gesture of despair. 'What a fool he was to get himself mixed up with these people. He really wasn't up to it.'

'Right,' I said eventually. 'I'm not quite sure where we go from here.'

'Well,' she said helpfully, 'I shall tell Adrian that you are lending a hand and hope he gets in touch with you, but surely the Italian police have more chance of laying their hands on the killer than you have?'

I paused in mid-breath. 'You'll tell Adrian,' I repeated slowly. 'I don't understand. Adrian's dead.'

'No, not that one,' she said with in an exasperated tone, as if she were addressing a half-wit. 'The real one.'

'"The real one."' I was beginning to lose my grasp on reality. I took a deep breath.

'Look, Faustina,' I said, my sense of linguistic decorum flying out of the window in the vehemence of my surprise, 'either I've lost what few marbles I had, or we've got our wires seriously crossed. You know, *fili incrociati* and all that. Now tell me exactly what you mean by "telling Adrian".'

'What do you mean, "what you mean"?' she replied, in the same exasperated tone. 'Adrian and I are in hiding. I am here in Bologna, he is – elsewhere, shall we say. When you have gone, I shall telephone him for a conversation. I cannot express myself more plainly than that.'

'Are we talking about the same person? Adrian Carrick, who part-owns and part-runs the Galleria Assunta in Fondamenta Venier in Venice? That's who we're talking about, am I right?'

'Yes, of course, Inspector. My partner.   Look, this is ridiculous. Who else could we be talking about?'

'We could be talking about the schoolteacher who was killed in Worcestershire in England two and a half weeks ago, that's who.'

'Ah,' she said contemptuously, 'he's not important. What do I care for him? He's nobody.'

I looked at her. There was not a trace of amusement on her face, which I could now see since her scarf had fallen away under the impulse of her irritation with my stupidity.

'We,' she said, '– well, Orlandina, actually – saw a paragraph in a London newspaper that Adrian Carrick had died in tragic circumstances – apparently by suicide. We knew then, without a doubt, that our enemies had made a mistake in assassinating the wrong Adrian Carrick but that it would be only a matter of time before they realised their error. For the moment, therefore, we are lying low. I don't know what we shall do in the long run.' A look of hopelessness absorbed her features.

I sat there, mute with stupefaction. There were two Adrian Carricks. The letters to the MC Gallery in Birmingham had betrayed the confusion between the two. I wheedled the story out of Faustina, although she knew only half of it, she said; the other half was guess-work. Orlandina had been told to contact Adrian Carrick in England. She had lost the contact address. Rather than admit her incompetence, she had consulted international lists of art-dealers and come up with a Carrick in Birmingham. Before noticing or being able to rectify her mistake, she had sent two more letters to Maurice's gallery, but since she still worked for Faustina, the mistake was never, presumably, discovered, or, if discovered, forgiven. Her misunderstanding had completely thrown me – and Maurice – and skewed our investigation irreparably. My days in Venice and Bologna had been completely wasted: time, energy and money poured wretchedly down the drain. I was shattered.

I sat there for a time trying to master my stupefaction. It then dawned on me that the investigation was now impossibly ambiguous. On the one hand, I could suppose that the killer, hired by Carrick's – Faustina's Carrick's – enemies, had made the same mistake as we had, only in reverse: he had attacked schoolteacher Carrick rather than the art-dealer Carrick he was meant to have killed. This would mean that the whole Italian 'connection' was completely irrelevant to my inquiry. On the other hand, there was no Italian connection at all: it was a mirage created by Orlandina's foolish error. Schoolteacher Carrick was murdered by an English contract killer, and art-dealer Carrick had taken fright because, reading about it in a British newspaper, he had jumped to the mistaken conclusion that the victim was meant to be he. There was even a third possibility: that the hired killer had deliberately targeted schoolteacher Carrick in order to frighten art-dealer Carrick and bring him into line. I am unsure what philosophers mean by 'disambiguation', but they *should* mean that detective inspectors have an uncomplicated, logical method of cutting through tangles of evidence and appearance. Perhaps I should engage in a bit of philosophy. On the other hand, although I had made a mistake, no one – least of all you, Kindly Reader - could assert that it was anything but an honest one.

Seven

There was nothing more I could do that night, but first thing in the morning, after a coffee and a croissant at a bar on my way into the city centre, I telephoned DCI Maxwell, explained my predicament and obtained his permission to return to Switzerland to interview Geela on my way back to Worcester. This would be my first time of meeting her, and I knew that 'interview' was an overstatement for the few questions I thought I should put to her. I was back on the train, therefore, but this time bound for Geneva. Taking a taxi to the Avenue Appia, in the Pregny area of the city, I asked to be dropped off at the Petit Château Rouge, which was an overblown town-house with a few towers and turrets and pretensions to gracious living. I am probably unfair: this may have been the duchess's fifth residence down in order of importance, occupied for a few weeks a year only, but maintained all the year round by an extensive staff of well-paid acolytes. I hoped that Geela could be released from her duties for a few minutes' conversation, and my request was granted without a murmur.

Geela and I weighed each other up, in the genteelest possible way, as we sat in a parlour somewhere on the ground floor. She was, if I judged her fairly, self-possessed; I was, well, not exactly nervous, but unsure of my ground. The truth of the matter is that I was not convinced that she could help, and even if she could, that she could help us materially. Was I simply reminding the poor girl of something she would much rather forget; dragging up an unpleasant experience when the proper course of action would be to let it slide into oblivion?

'Miss Purdew,' I began, 'I don't know whether you are aware that we are now treating Mr Carrick's death as murder.'

'Murder? But I thought –'

'Yes, well, since the inquest, a witness has come forward testifying that he saw a man walking with Mr Carrick minutes before his death.

We have not traced this man, but we believe him to be a professional killer hired by an unknown party to get Mr Carrick out of the way. My coming here today does not imply in any way that we think you are implicated – I wish you to be quite clear on that score - but you may have a suggestion or two to make of which we are not yet aware.'

'Well, Inspector, I should much rather put the whole episode behind me. I liked Mr Carrick very much, but his death and the events leading up to it were a great trial, and I don't really want to dwell on them; but I'll help if I can, of course.'

'Good. We're a bit stuck at the moment because the one motive for his murder that we thought we had we have no longer got.' I gave Geela a brief explanation of what I had been doing for the last three days, making out, heavens forgive me, that my mistake was not just understandable but forced on me by another's incompetence.

'What you need, Inspector,' she said promptly, 'is a bit of Popper.'

'Do I? Tell me about Popper, then.'

'Well, Popper elaborated his theory of trial and error – or, as he preferred to call it, conjecture and refutation – after reading Hume. Hume said that induction as a philosophical or scientific method cannot be logically justified: theories can never be inferred from observation.'

'Explain.'

'OK. For example, Hume argued that the repetition of an event, for example, sunrise, induces in us, psychologically, an acceptance of an underlying law, namely, in this case, that the sun rises every morning and sets at night. Popper realised that Hume had involved himself in a logical impossibility. Repeated events don't impose a law *on* us: we interpret events in terms of laws imposed *by* us.'

'Yes, I think I follow that.'

'Popper then used Kant to elaborate this view, that all scientific laws are products of our innate mental equipment: we need to find "regularities", as Popper calls them, in order to make sense of our environment, so we impose them on the "facts": we arrange and order and "explain" facts in terms of structures and laws.'

'So what's your point?'

'I'm getting there, Inspector!' Geela said, almost as if she were addressing one of her dimmer charges. 'Where Kant went wrong was to suppose that the innate structures, which are like a net or filter through which we view everything and on the basis of which we pigeon-hole the various items of our experience, are immutable. No, said Popper, the intelligent scientist or philosopher works with the laws he finds to hand but *tests* them, hoping to be able to prove or disprove them and so advance his knowledge.'

'And so?'

'My, Inspector, you are impatient! Well, Popper's conclusion is that science and philosophy make progress by throwing up conjectures and then trying to refute them. This means that the proper approach to problems is to look round for a solution and then to test the solution. Popper uses the two words "dogmatism" and "critique". The first is the attitude characteristic of primitives and children – and plenty of others! – who fit facts to a preconceived schema; the second is that of the educated person who is cautious and analytical, treading carefully and weighing the pros and cons. All things must be subjected to the cool light of reason. I should tell you, here, Inspector, that I owe all this to Mr Carrick: he was brilliant at making complicated things understandable.'

'I see. And how can *I*, a plodding policeman, use Popper?'

'What you need to do, Inspector, is to conjecture, to come up with surmises, however wild, and then submit them to rigorous testing.' If this is how philosophy encouraged eighteen-year-olds to express themselves, I was all in favour!

'OK,' I said, 'you come up with a conjecture, if you're so smart!'

'Here's two, then, Inspector. Firstly, a woman who loves Mr Carrick sees him and me together enjoying a quiet tea in Pershore and embracing before and afterwards, and she is so jealous she determines to punish him – a sort of twentieth-century Medea. Alternatively,' Geela continued, 'a man sees Mr Carrick embracing me and enjoying with me a quiet cup of tea and a scone in seemingly friendly circumstances, and is driven insane with jealousy, because he regards me as his possession – a sort of twentieth-century Orlando Furioso.'

'My goodness, we are well educated! If I had any daughters, they'd be inscribed at Grant College without more ado – only perhaps policemen's daughters couldn't afford the fees! By the way, did you get into Exeter?'

'I did, but I've decided to take a year out.'

'Well, congratulations on your acceptance. What will you read?'

'Business studies with French.'

'I see, good. Now, anything else spring to mind with regard to Mr Carrick's death? Any more – conjectures?' I put her this question somewhat facetiously, I confess. Geela responded in kind.

'Well, seeing as how you ask, Inspector, what about this? Imagine that a matron had professed her deep, undying love for Mr Carrick – "Darling, you must be mine! I cannot live without you! Say you will be mine, or I shall feed you to the birds" – and he spurned her because of the love of his dead wife. That would be very romantic! Or try this. Mr Carrick was well-known for his rambles in the countryside. What if on one of them he saw something he ought not to have seen? Perhaps he knows who committed some ghastly crime and has to be removed before he can blab to the police. Or this: someone else wants Mr Carrick's job at Grant, so he – or, of course, she – removes Mr Carrick just in time to land his job for the September term. Or this: membership of a gang in Pershore – does that sound very unlikely? OK, let's say a gang in downtown Merseyside – depends on committing a murder which is not identified as murder within three weeks of its committal; so some aspiring gangster pushes Mr Carrick into a quarry and then, after the coroner's verdict, claims his right to membership. And have you considered whether it might not have been an accident? The man you tell me was seen walking with Mr Carrick minutes before his death was a friend, and the two were enjoying a companionable walk arm in arm. Adrian says to his friend, "Ooh, let me show you a rare variety of agrimony that grows only in this one quarry in the whole world," and they walk over to view this rare plant. Unfortunately Mr Carrick, in his eagerness to point it out, slips and disappears over the edge. The friend then does a bunk in case he's accused of murder.'

'Stop, Geela, stop!' I noticed that, in my admiration for this personable young woman, I had slipped into familiar mode – for the second time in as many days. Dear, oh, dear, I was losing my grip on the principle of chivalrous demeanour at all times! 'And you're suggesting that Professor Popper would approve of all this?'

'Conjecture, and refute if you can: that's the rule, Inspector! You can't go wrong!'

I was beginning to see why Adrian Carrick could be smitten with this young person: she was fun to be with.

'Right, let's be serious for a minute,' I said. 'Tell me: how do you feel about things now – now that nearly three weeks have passed?'

'I was very upset at the time: I left the tea-rooms in turmoil. I'm only eighteen, Inspector, and probably not a very mature eighteen, in some ways. I looked ahead and envisaged another meeting with Mr Carrick in twelve months' time: I couldn't face it! What would I say? How would I feel? What would *he* say? And then when news of his death came out, I was sad – sad for the end of a good life. To cap it all, his death was judged to be suicide because I had left him sitting there, alone, facing the teapot and the jam! The coroner was very kind in his remarks, but I was left wondering whether I had a man's suicide on my conscience. I struggled with this, and I have kept on having to tell myself that I couldn't have acted otherwise. Now you come along and tell me it was murder. It's all too much, Inspector.' Her lip quivered. 'That's why I'm glad to be abroad, in different surroundings, and being worked hard.'

'Yes, I can understand that you haven't found it easy. Still, you've managed a few jokes today.'

'Oh, I'll get over it, I'm sure. It'll just take a bit of time, that's all. I shall need time to absorb in particular the idea of murder.'

I thanked her very much for her time and for her invaluable contribution to the investigation and expressed the hope that we should meet again.

When I rejoined my colleague, Sergeant Spooner, in Britain, I naturally gave him a brief account of the time I had wasted in Venice and St.Gallen and assured him that I now purposed to continue the inquiry tenaciously, starting from a firm philosophical basis. When he asked what precisely I meant by that enigmatical remark, I outlined my conversation with Geela and then added:

'Of course, we have been working by trial and error – sorry, by conjecture and refutation – since always, but it's nice to know we have official backing, as it were. To be told so so prettily was a bonus. However, to work. We shall undertake to contact Geela's boyfriend, if she had or has one; and to discover whether Carrick had a serious lady-friend. One thing Geela overlooked was Carrick's will: we need to see where his money went. We shall also, I suppose, have to ask the headmistress how and with whom she proposes to fill the gap in her staff. Some of Geela's suggestions are too fanciful, however. I mean, I don't see how Carrick's death could have been an accident, as she – "conjectures". We know somebody borrowed a car via various intermediaries to be present at Little Comberton on the day in question: that is not the action of a man who just happens to be taking a stroll with the victim of an accident. I want you, therefore, Sergeant, to contact Carrick's lawyer about his will and then to find out about any lady-friends Carrick might have had. In the meantime, I shall see Mrs Howard and Geela's parents. Somewhere, somehow, we must uncover a motive for murder. Right, jump to it, my lad! We mean business.'

Carrick's lawyers were the firm of Church, Bell, Ringer & Co. (I kid you not) in the High Street, Pershore, and this account of the conversation that formed the substance of Spooner's visit there I owe, naturally, to Spooner. He spoke with Mr Robert Bell.

'Good morning, Sir. We are investigating the death of Mr Carrick, which we have reason to believe was suspicious, and we wondered whether you could help us with his will.'

'Certainly, Sergeant, I retrieved it from our files as soon as the receptionist told me you were on your way. I do not think you will find in it anything remarkable, beyond a certain old fashioned style he insisted on.' Saying which, he handed the will over to Spooner. This in substance is what he read:

> In the name of God Amen I Adrian Percy Carrick of Little Comberton in the parish of Pershore diocese of Worcester being of sound mind and body and in the sixtieth year of my age make this my last Will and Testament in manner and form following First I give and bequeath my soul into the hands of Almighty God my Maker and Redeemer and my body to be buried with that of my beloved wife Calandra Monica in Pershore Cemetery, Defford Road, Pershore
>
> Item I give and bequeath to Phyllida Cruickshank the sum of fifty pounds as a token of my affection and esteem
>
> Item I give and bequeath to Geela Purdew the sum of twenty-five pounds as a token of my affection and esteem
>
> Item I give and bequeath to my nieces Barbara Carrick and Bernadette Haslehurst and to my nephews Vincent Carrick and Cornelius Haslehurst fifty pounds apiece as I wish them well

Also I will there be made the day of my burial or as soon thereafter as proves possible and convenient one substantial dinner for my neighbours and friends that will come to it

The rest of all my goods not bequeathed my debts paid legacies and funeral expenses discharged I freely give and bequeath in equal shares to my son Maurice Rovert Carrick and to my daughter Frances Shannon Haslehurst whom I make joint Executors of this my last Will and Testament These being Witnesses etc

It was signed on 1 July 1974.

Spooner told me that there were various conditions attached, notably: if either of his children predeceased him, his or her share went to their offspring; if they both predeceased him, the bulk of the estate was to be divided equally between a dozen charities, with specific substantial bequests to the nephews and nieces.

'This will is perfectly in order, Sergeant,' the lawyer, commented, 'if a little, shall I say, whimsical. There is nothing here unexpected or untoward.'

'Do you happen to know who Phyllida Cruickshank is?'

'No, I don't, Sergeant. But the sum bequeathed is quite modest, a token really, nothing to get worked up about.'

Spooner – I am still purveying to you the gist of his report – then telephoned Frances Haslehurst at her book-bindery in Hereford and asked about the unknown beneficiary. Mrs Haselehurt understood Phyllida Cruickshank to be a near-neighbour of her father's at Little Comberton. Her, Spooner duly went to see. There was, he thought, something feline about Mrs Cruickshank, widow: physically slinky and smooth, personally wily and determined. He knew better, however, than to let his first impressions govern his more considered assessment; except that further acquaintance simply reinforced his first impressions! She lived in a small house on one of the newer developments in the village, a modern, nondescript property in a colourless cul-de-sac. She seemed to Spooner to be a little uncertain about the nature of the welcome she should offer him, but, as she absorbed the nature of his business with her, she relented, so to speak, and invited him in. She seemed thereafter to be glad of the company. Over a cup of tea, she explained her circumstances and how she had come to know Adrian Carrick.

'It's like this, Sergeant,' she said. 'I married a man quite a bit my senior. I was not exactly in love with him, but I was well into my thirties and thinking that, alas, I was destined to remain a spinster all my days, when John came along and proposed. I accepted, because a relationship based on mutual regard, although not ideal, seemed preferable to a lifetime's solitude. I didn't regret the marriage, although I confess I was disappointed that he wasn't as well off as I had been led to believe. We jogged along satisfactorily enough, but I confess to you, Sergeant – are you a married man, Sergeant?'

'Yes, happily I am, Mrs Cruickshank.'

'Oh, do call me Phyl: everyone does. Then you will know what I mean when I say that I was hungry for love, real love. I had married, but what I got was not what I had dreamed of as a girl. All my own fault, of course: I had gone into the marriage with my eyes wide open, but under the pressure of natural forces I was powerless to deal with.' Here, perversely, she narrowed her eyes, and she took on, in Spooner's fancy, the traits of a particularly watchful leopardess. Her green eyes and lithe body curled up in her armchair were somehow menacing.

'John was kind to me, but we had very little money and couldn't afford any of the things I had set my heart on: foreign travel, a swanky car, a big house, rich friends … Stupid, really. I know it. I know it now, I knew it then, but a lifetime's maidenhood was just not to be thought of. After ten years John died. I was left alone again, and just as poor as before. I had not found love, but I feared I never then should. I was in my forties, still quite good-looking, I told myself, reasonably good company, not hard to please, open to offers; but I never met anyone who meant anything to me. Perhaps I was choosier than I had imagined. You see, this time, I wanted to get it right. Then Adrian came along.' She stopped, with a dreamy look in her expressive eyes. She purred in contemplation of the object of her desire.

'How did he come along?' Spooner asked, by way of prompt, I suppose. Her mood changed instantly to one of anger. She flexed her claws and snarled, with her upper lip curled and her teeth bared.

'Get on with your story, Spooner,' I said in exasperation. 'Just cut out all the fancy footwork.'

'Yes sir! I'm only trying to convey a feel for my interview with Mrs Cruickshank. As I say, she sat there, curled up, the image of feline fury. Sorry, Sir: I just can't help myself!'

'He fell for a slip of a schoolgirl,' Mrs Cruickshank continued, 'and threw himself off a cliff. I ask you, Sergeant. Just when happiness was in my grasp! You have no conception of how angry and bitter I am.' A wave of grief engulfed her.

'Tell me how you and he came to meet - Phyl,' Spooner said after a pause.

'Simple, so simple, and yet so typical of the man. I was in my front garden, struggling to uproot a small tree that had outgrown its position. He happened to be passing by and stopped to remonstrate with me. "Now stop that at once, Young Lady," he said. "Young Lady": I was in my fifties, for heaven's sake! "You'll do yourself a mischief, and that's just silly. Give me a few minutes to change, and I'll be back round to do the job for you." "No, no," I replied, I couldn't dream of putting you to the trouble." "No trouble whatever," he said, "I enjoy gardening. It'll be a pleasure." So he came back round a few minutes later, true to his word, we had a cup of tea after the tree was dispatched, and that's how it started.'

'May I just ask, Mrs – Phyl, whether he reciprocated your regard for him.'

'There you have me, Sergeant: I don't know. I was frightened of upsetting the relationship, of seeming to hurry, of pushing him into a corner. I never said anything about my love for him, but he must have known what I felt; he must have done. The only information he ever dropped in my hearing was that he grieved continually for his wife, but I didn't need him to tell me that. I was content to let the relationship jog along, compensating in my imagination for the reality that it still lacked.'

'Mrs – Phyl, what I am about to say may come as a surprise to you: we now think that Adrian Carrick was the victim of a contract killing.'

'What! no, he can't have been! Who on earth would wish to murder gentle, kind-hearted, clever Adrian? No, you've got it wrong, Sergeant, quite wrong, you must have.'

Spooner outlined our reasons for thinking so. She sat there bewildered. After a suitable pause, Spooner asked whether this intelligence opened up any other possibilities concerning the motive behind Carrick's death. Nothing came to mind, she said – or rather, she intimated with a shake of her head in silent denial. Spooner left the leopardess to her grief and bewilderment.

Eight

Spooner's graphic report is now followed by my own much more pedestrian account. You may remember – if you have not dozed off on the cushions or on the pillows – that I was delegated (by myself, in an equitable division of labour with my sergeant) to prosecute our inquiries with Mrs Howard, headmistress of Grant College, and with Geela's parents. Mrs Howard wondered whether I should mind squeezing my visit in between a staff-meeting and lunch: the term was starting, girls were arriving, parents were wishing to see her: the usual frenzied activity that accompanies the opening of a school year, even though Grant imposed a veneer of order and *sang-froid* on such unavoidable occasions.

The school, a former country seat of the Grant family, lay to the west of the village of Bricklehampton and was announced by ornamental gates on the road. It was a late eighteenth-century pile, Adamesque, with a portico, large windows, some decoration in the stone-work, and a gracious if somewhat stolid air. The drive cut through parkland, where deer grazed placidly, and then through a short copse at an angle to the main drive before debouching dramatically at the front. Parking was forbidden (sensibly) along the esplanade, but space to the side of the mansion was reserved for visitors. When I announced my arrival, a prefect, on hand to welcome new girls, was made available to accompany me up the grand staircase, through the magnificent Central Hall – unusually, this space is elliptical, with a gallery all the way round and the ceiling open to a decorated skylight – to the headmistress's office on the first floor, overlooking the front lawns of the school. The room was large, comfortably, even opulently, furnished. One could hear, as we talked, drifting up from below through the open windows, the arrival of the first girls in taxis and cars, and the excited chatter, and the bump of trunks and cases, and the tears; within, however, all was decorum and restraint.

I began by avowing to Mrs Howard that our inquiry had advanced but little in the week since I had been put on the case, largely because of a false trail -- laid by an inept and bungling junior in a small art-gallery in a Venetian back-street, except that that was a detail I omitted -- but I became more animated (I confess this to you, who are witnessing in the course of this narrative some of Wickfield's many weaknesses) when I gave her a summary of my conversation with Geela.

'However,' I said, resuming my habitual business-like tone, 'my main purpose in speaking to you is to ask you how you have filled Mr Carrick's post at such short notice.'

Mrs Howard looked at me askance. 'I'm not sure I see the relevance of that,' she said, with (I thought) needless acidity. I could hardly admit that Geela had planted the idea in my mind, but I did not stretch the truth when I said suavely,

'Well, you see, Mrs Howard, it is possible that Mr Carrick's death was not suicide but murder, engineered to make way for another incumbent, with who knows what ultimate intention.'

'All I can say is, Inspector, that you have a very tortuous mind if that's how you operate.'

'That's as may be, Mrs Howard, but you will appreciate that we are bound to follow up all possible threads, whether they lead us anywhere or not.'

'Well, I apologise if I sounded abrupt, Inspector. The first day of a school year is always a little bit fraught, even in the best regulated establishments: so much to go wrong, you know, and so many uncertainties with new teachers, new girls and new parents, and all the mishaps that affect the travelling public, and new systems in place, and so forth. Take no notice of me, but I should appreciate it if we could come to the point.'

'Then please tell me whom you have engaged to fill the Spanish/philosophy vacancy and how you engaged him or her.'

'Taking Mr Carrick's place is an experienced woman in her fifties, who has moved down here with her husband's job, from somewhere in the Midlands -- Solihull, if memory serves me - now lives in Evesham. I was on the point of advertising nationally, knowing that in all likelihood I should, at that stage, be able to recruit nothing but a probationer, when she pops up spontaneously, explains her situation and asks whether there might not be a job going. We were apparently one of four or five schools within commuting distance to whom she had offered her services – which included French and pastoral care – but we were the first with a suitable vacancy. She had perfectly respectable, indeed glowing, testimonials from two previous schools, and I was very happy to engage her on the spot, particularly as I was very busy at the time fielding questions from parents anxious about their daughters' examination results. Now if there's nothing else, Inspector ...'

Mrs Purdew – Geela's mother - worked for BBC Hereford and Worcester in their Worcester offices, and it was there that I made my next visit. She was able to receive me after a short delay, and I hastened to assure her that I should require her attention for a few minutes only. Her daughter closely resembled her, although, naturally, the mother's good looks were maturer and perhaps more subtle. I told Mrs Purdew that I had had the good fortune to meet her daughter in Switzerland three days before, and I congratulated her on rearing so engaging a daughter. Mrs Purdew was clearly pleased by my spontaneous tribute! I also told her that Geela had volunteered a few suggestions – 'conjectures' in Popperian parlance! – and that I was following some of them up as part of our wider consideration of the case.

'The inquest into Mr Carrick's death put quite a strain on Geela, you know, Inspector. She was very fond of Mr Carrick, and despite the coroner's every effort, she felt a heavy weight of responsibility.'

'I can tell you, Mrs Purdew, that we are now fairly certain that Mr Carrick's death was murder –' she looked very surprised – 'and I told Geela this. I think you will find that she is much happier about her role now. Well, really, she doesn't seem to have had one.'

'So what brings you to these offices, Inspector?' she asked dryly.

'Well, semi-humorously, in the course of our conversation, Geela suggested that perhaps a male admirer of hers had resented seeing her with Mr Carrick on that fatal Tuesday and had determined to remove him from the scene: not very likely, I admit, but I'm asking you about such a person because we still haven't got a full grasp of the circumstances in which Carrick found himself when he was done to death. I forgot to pursue this question when I was with Geela.'

'I see. Well, attendance at a girls' school doesn't exactly facilitate congress with the opposite sex: I think that's partly, or even mainly, the point of it! but Geela knew plenty of boys from her previous school and through general socialising in the holidays.'

'Any particular ones?'

'Well, two spring to mind: Jason Rossiter and Desmond Hay, both Pershore boys, but I really think that the idea that either of them could have murdered Mr Carrick is ridiculous, if you don't mind my saying so, Inspector.' She threw me a quizzical, not to say incredulous, glance. 'They're both younger than Geela, a little bit anyway, and as far as I can see, there is nothing serious between either of them and Geela.'

'Yes, well, I admit that the chances of a useful lead are remote, but we need to follow ideas up in case they lead to something else. I should be grateful for their addresses, if you have them. Do you know these two youths?'

'Yes, both nice, well-mannered boys. They're pupils at King's in Worcester.'

'I see. Just before I go, Mrs Purdew, could you enlighten me on why you chose the name Geela for your daughter? It's intrigued me.'

'Yes, it means Eternal Joy.'

'Is there such a thing? Not this side of death, surely!'

'Well, we thought it a very suitable way to start her life: she will bring us eternal joy, we thought, and we wish eternal joy for her. The name doesn't actually come in the Bible, but it is Hebrew – not that that has anything particularly to do with why we chose it!'

'Thank you, Mrs Purdew: very commendable sentiments. I hope I shan't have to trouble you again.'

It was a pleasure to drive back then to Worcester to visit King's, to ask for permission to have a word with the two boys in question. I thought it preferable to see the boys separately. I explained to the headmaster that I wanted to ask them a couple of routine questions - a few minutes of their time would suffice – in connection with Adrian Carrick's death. He knew of the matter, of course: it is not every day of the week that a sitting member of school staff is the subject of a coroner's inquest. I had trouble, however, in convincing him that two of his boys could know anything that was in the slightest degree pertinent! Despite the fact that authority and power sit easily on me, I was embarrassed when the boys were summoned separately at the headmaster's bidding from whatever duties round the place they were attending to, but I secretly agreed with him that it was in the highest degree unlikely that they would have anything to contribute. Although both lads turned out to be a year younger than Geela, they were both particularly mature for their age (I thought).

Jason Rossiter was a big-framed, curly-headed youth with a bronze complexion and the build of a prop forward. How competent he was at his studies I could not, of course, tell. He told me that he had seen nothing of Geela over the holidays, since (as I knew) she had been abroad, and he had worked in his father's factory. The last time he had seen her was at the Sixth-Form ball held at Grant in May. Did he know that one of Geela's teachers had met his death three weeks ago?

'Yes, Inspector, I heard that: my mum told me. King's and Grant are fairly close, you see, being the two best private schools in the area, so news from one reaches the other pretty quickly, even in holiday time.'

'Now you say that the last time you saw Geela was in May. I understood from her mother that you and Geela got on pretty well together.'

'Yes, Sir.'

'And yet you made no effort to contact here once the holidays had started.'

'Who said I made no effort? I did ring her, but we couldn't find a date which suited us both, so that was that.'

'And when do you expect to see her again?'

'Heaven knows, Inspector. With Geela abroad, and me, worse luck, stuck here, I may not see her again until Christmas. Why?'

'No why. Thank you, Jason: nice to talk to you.'

I could not see Jason getting so jealous of Carrick as to wish to murder him. Now for young Master Hay.

'Good afternoon, Inspector. Thank you for saving me from mothering some of the new boys.'

'Oh, I've no doubt you'll have to make up for it somehow! Take a pew, Desmond. Let's get down to business.'

Hay was a spare, gangly youth with a noticeable rudiment of beard and a particularly adult and benign countenance. If looks were anything to go by, he never caused trouble in class – or probably anywhere else.

'I was just telling Jason Rossiter that we think Mr Carrick's death three weeks ago – you know about it, I daresay – was murder and that a particular circle of girls at Grant might just conceivably have something to do with it, however remotely. By that I don't mean anything *directly* to do with it, I hasten to add. You do know, I suppose, that the inquest gave a verdict of suicide on the grounds that Mr Carrick was disturbed about losing the friendship of Geela Purdew?'

'Yes, I did know that, Sir.'

'You know Geela well, I'm told.'

'Yes, I've known her all my life.'

'How close was your relationship, may I ask?'

'I'm not quite sure what you mean, Inspector. We were good friends, that's it. Nothing else to say.'

'Could you see your relationship developing?'

'Developing? How developing? Now that Geela has got a place at uni, our ways in life are already diverging. We'll both make new friends, what else can happen?'

'Did you know about Mr Carrick's high regard for Geela?'

'Yes. Well, I knew they got on very well together.'

'And you knew they had a final meeting in Pershore four days before Mr Carrick died?'

'Yes, it was in all the papers. From what I gather, there was absolutely no attempt at concealment. I mean, you can't have tea in the Abbey Tea Rooms and not expect to be seen, probably by half the town, can you?'

'*You* didn't happen to see them, did you?'

'No, but my Mum did.'

'And?'

'And nothing. There they were, having a cup of tea. Hardly noteworthy, Sir, if I may say so. Why do you ask?'

I found myself forced to repeat my less than elegant untruth to Jason Rossiter:

'No why.'

Satisfied that I had fulfilled my duty in seeing the two youths, I concluded that they constituted, however noble their character, however promising their future and whatever global renown they might achieve in years to come, one small cul-de-sac as far as my inquiry was concerned.

I returned to Worcester, ensconced myself in my battered office chair, and, I freely confess, did absolutely nothing for the next ten minutes except sit blankly. I just could not see my way forward. Eventually I summoned Spooner, asked him for his report – which I have summarised for you above - filled him in on my own day's work and invited him to summarise the case so far, to see whether anything – the tiniest thing - occurred to either of us.

'Well, Sir,' he began, 'the week since we have been on the case has been spent exploring – necessarily so, Sir, since we knew none of the people involved and none of the background, but I think we have made some progress. Actually, Sir, if I may say so, I think we've done quite well!' I groaned: had I succeeded in deceiving even my own sergeant?

'Yes, go on, Spooner, I'm listening.'

'The facts strongly suggested that Mr Carrick had done away with himself, and that was indeed the finding of the coroner's court, but in the very first day of our inquiry we established that he had been pushed over the edge of the quarry by a hired killer. In my view, Sir, that conclusion is rock solid. We know who the killer is, and it's only a matter of time before he's caught. In the meantime, we need to know who hired him and why; that's the tricky bit. After that, you went to Venice, Bologna and St.Gallen and uncovered the shadowy and unsavoury activities of a Carrick double. On your way back to the United Kingdom, you interviewed young Miss Purdew but, with all respect, Sir, came away with nothing new, enchanting, articulate, learned and pretty though she apparently was.'

'Yes, thank you, Sergeant, I get the message: the young woman's a siren and should not be let loose on the male population – not even inspectors of police are immune!'

'Now today, Sir,' Spooner continued smoothly, with a nod of acquiescence, 'we've been particularly active. Between us, we've interviewed Mr Carrick's lawyer, his lady admirer Mrs Cruickshank, his former headmistress and his replacement at Grant College, Geela's mother and two of Geela's male friends. Our conclusions at this stage may be purely negative, but all this work has enabled us to exclude certain obvious options. There is no sign that Carrick was done away with by a business associate, for the simple reason that he had none, by a jealous female acquaintance, by a jealous male acquaintance, by someone after his job or his money, or by someone he'd double-crossed or otherwise offended. Now that doesn't leave us with many alternatives, but it's surely cleared the ground, Sir?'

'Right, what alternatives does it leave?'

'The first is rather vague: Carrick knew something and had to be silenced. How one begins to find that out I'm not quite sure, Sir, since he seems not to have confided in anyone on that score.'

'What else?'

'The second is outlandish. It is that Mr & Mrs Purdew feared for their daughter's virtue or safety and decided to eliminate Adrian Carrick.'

'Surely there would have been less drastic methods than murder, though?'

'That's what I mean, Sir: it's outlandish.'

'Yes, I agree, but as you have been talking, another idea has been gradually forming in my mind. You see, Sergeant, you have on me the wonderful effect of stimulating my – however modest – conjectural skills. Will you bear with me for a moment while I think aloud? Let's go back to the devious Mr Art Cartel Carrick in his Venice flat. He has fallen foul of someone – this is me speculating; he lies low, he and his captivating Faustina; he concocts a scheme to save his skin not just in the short term but in the long term. He decides to kill Mr Schoolteacher Carrick! It doesn't matter to him whether the coroner's verdict is suicide, murder, death by misadventure or natural causes – or anything else: liquidation by Martian aliens, for example, or being trampled to death by a herd of woolly-haired mammoths - the important thing is that Carrick's death is reported in the press. The letters from Venice of two years ago were deliberately planted to make a connection between a Mr Adrian Carrick in the Midlands of

England and an art-dealer in Venice, ready for the time when their full use could be exploited. The result of this machination is that everybody – that is, everybody who matters - believes that Venetian art-dealer Carrick is dead, pushed over the edge of a quarry in the course of a walk on Bredon Hill in darkest Worcestershire. Art-dealer Carrick then adopts another identity, spirits his savings away from his bank and settles in, I don't know, Barcelona or Ragusa as, let us say, Sir Millington Swashbuckle and sets himself up in the same business or begins another venture entirely: money-laundering, forgery, a financial scam, a fish-and-chip shop, a commercial dry-cleaner's or what-have-you. What happens to the fair Faustina I'm not sure. She might or might not be included in the disappearing act, depending on the depth of Carrick's loyalty to her. Now that, young Spooner, is a hypothesis - sorry, a conjecture – we can work with! What do you think?'

I sat back, rather pleased with myself, and doubtless showing it on my handsome face.

'Yes, Sir, I think that's rather good!'

'Thank you, Sergeant. Can my autograph wait until I've succeeded in finding my pen? What we need to do now, then, according to our friend Professor Popper, is to test this conjecture in the hope of refuting it. If we cannot refute it, it stands as the most likely hypothesis; I think I have got that right. It now becomes imperative to locate Mr Art Gallery Carrick in his hidey-hole, and for that we shall need to return to Venice to bend the ear of the lovely but clumsy, or perhaps not so clumsy, Orlandina. I'm beginning to enjoy this case, I must say!'

Nine

Because we were dealing with a cunning and dangerous criminal, I obtained the DCI's permission for Spooner to accompany me to Venice. Once installed in the Hotel delle Streghe – and I am glad to be able to relate to you that the manager remembered me instantly – we sauntered off to the Galleria Assunta to renew acquaintance with the delectable Orlandina. To our mortification, there was a piece of card pinned to the inside of the door: *Chiuso fino a nuovo avviso.* For the gallery to be closed until further notice was vexing beyond endurance. We had made the long journey only to be thwarted at the very first portal. Not only had Faustina and Carrick gone into hiding; Orlandina had followed them, who knew whither! I was not to be so easily baulked of my prey. It was by then too late in the day to further our inquiries, but first thing in the morning, we returned to Mestre, picked up a connection to Bologna and made our way back to the seedy bar where I rendez-vous'd with Faustina the previous week. The barman was not the same one as I had noticed on my first visit: he was overweight, large, low-browed, unshaven and quite villainous to look at. (Please note that these remarks are an impartial comment on his *appearance*: I say nothing about the man behind the appearance, who could have been an exemplary husband, father and lover of the poor.) I decided to take him by the horns (so to speak). Waving my stamped letter of authority under his nose, staring at him firmly and taking a shot at random, I told him, in my silkiest Italian, that he would be run in for infringing this or that provision of Italian law unless he told me what he knew about Faustina, whom I described in as accurate a way as I could, scarf and all. He hesitated, saw from my furrowed brow and steely expression that I was in earnest, and finally volunteered the information that *la Signorina* Faustina might be found residing in rooms above a furniture restorer's further down the street. Releasing my (metaphorical) grip, I put down a 1000 lire note, as an earnest against future assistance, led Spooner out of the bar and proceeded down the street for a few doors until we came to dingy premises cluttered with bits of chairs and tables and tatters of upholstery and advertising itself as *Da Gino*. Gino (I presumed it was he) pointed me wordlessly in the direction of a door on the street to the side of his premises, at which I rang an electric bell and waited. After a short while, a head shrouded in a scarf appeared at the window above our heads and instantly retreated. I concluded that the fair owner of the head had recognised me for whom I was and for the authority that I represented and was even then descending the stairs to open up to us. I was accurate in my diagnosis. She remained hidden behind the door as she opened it, with the consequence that we were left with insufficient room to negotiate the gap, but eventually we gained access and preceded Faustina up the stairs. We heard bolts being drawn after us.

When we were seated in her darkened room, I asked whether she would mind, for the sergeant's sake, speaking in English.

'It is dangerous for me if you are seen here,' she muttered. 'Why did you not make rendez-vous as before?'

I explained that, since Orlandina was no longer at the gallery, we had had no choice but to trace her in Bologna.

'Orlandina not at the gallery? How can that be?'

'I have no idea,' I said truthfully, 'but we're here now, and that is all that matters. We need urgently to speak to Adrian Carrick, *Signorina*. Where can we find him?'

I prided myself that we had her cornered and she knew it. She had the grace not to hurry into speech.

'He does not exist, *Signori*.'

'He does not exist,' I repeated, stupidly. 'You must explain, *Signorina*, because I don't think I understand you.'

'Adrian Carrick is dead.' She said this without expression. 'There is only one Adrian Carrick, and he died in a quarry in Worcestershire.'

'But you yourself told me there was another one: your partner in the art gallery, the one you shared a flat with in Venice.'

'I wanted Adrian's memory to be kept pure and white. I did not wish his family or the police to know that he led a double life. I wanted him to go to his grave with his reputation *intatto* – how you say? intact.' Her English was falling apart under the strength of her emotion. 'So I invented a double so that Adrian could be laid to rest, with everyone thinking of him as a model schoolmaster and nothing else.'

'But Herr Fehrmann knows of him,' I objected.

'Yes, of course, Inspector: there is only one, and he knows him! They were partners.'

'And what's happened to Orlandina?'

'I left her in Venice, running the shop, because it is still my livelihood. So she is gone too! She is as afraid as I am. *Dio mio.*' She trembled on the edge of tears.

'And who killed Adrian? The same person you and now Orlandina are hiding from, obviously, but who is it? You must know.'

'I do know, but the knowledge itself is dangerous. We are up against serious *imbroglioni* - crooks who will stick at nothing. All I can do is run and hide until the danger is past.'

'And how will you know when that is?'

'I have a number to contact in a day or two, when I shall be told how much of a fine I have to pay for collaborating in a scam against the organisation.'

'Can you tell me what the scam was?'

'Adrian pretended to be a private buyer, always bid by phone, and bought works by Venetian artists at a low price because the dealers weren't bidding. He hoped to build up a modest collection to sell at a profit when the price when up. Someone must have rumbled him, heaven knows how.'

'And you think it was these people who arranged for Adrian's death in Worcestershire. How can you be so sure?'

'Because he had received an animal's heart in the post not so long ago.'

'And you know it was from them?'

'Who else could it have been from?'

'If you knew about this, why didn't you warn Adrian?'

'I did, but it was too late then. Once they've forewarned you, there's no way of avoiding your fate.'

'But if Adrian was expecting reprisals, why on earth did he go for a mid-morning stroll from home with a complete stranger?'

'I suppose because the killer said he wanted to discuss terms. "Let's go for a short walk while I tell you how the bosses will suspend the punishment under certain conditions. They want you on board, but there are certain things you must do first to satisfy them that the offence won't be repeated." Adrian might have fallen for that.   Or perhaps he didn't fall for it but refused to accept the conditions specified. *Chi lo sa*: who knows?'

'How did you and he meet, *Signorina*?'

'Some years ago, Adrian was on holiday in Venice, trying to get over his wife's death, and he was lonely. He told me that he loved the city – this was not his first visit – but on his own he tended to lack direction and focus and so spent the days wandering about rather aimlessly, responding to the whims of the moment. He would buy an all-day *vaporetto* ticket and ride up and down the Grand Canal. On one of these directionless journeys, we bumped into each other – literally – when I tripped on a rope and cannoned into him. He was kind enough to pick me up, we stopped to chat for a few minutes, and the result was a meal together that evening at a *pizzeria*. It went on from there. Our relationship was informal, even when he had engaged me as the active partner in his art gallery: no ties on either side. I used his room on the Fondamenta Venier, and he dropped in to stay from time to time, whenever his teaching duties permitted.'

'Right,' I said masterfully, determined to winkle essential information out of Faustina, 'so who are these people who threatened Adrian?'

'I daren't tell you!'

'You'll just have to. They're wanted for murder and goodness knows what else, and they need to be brought to justice.'

'What hope have you when the Italian authorities have not yet succeeded in assuring them to justice?' 'Assuring them to justice'? I thought that must mean bringing them to book, although I admit that the phrase was new to me. Despite further conversation and urging, she refused to yield; clearly she was more frightened of her Italian enemies than of me (but then my exterior person is particularly benign).

For reasons which I could not analyse, I was dissatisfied with Faustina's story: perhaps because I had attuned myself to the idea that there were two Adrian Carricks and that the one was using the other as camouflage, and I was not willing to let it go easily. Deciding therefore that Spooner and I should visit the immigration authorities, we walked down to the *Ufficio Immigrazione Comune di Venezia* in the Campo Santa Maria, a little to the north of St Mark's, stopping for refreshment on the way to fortify ourselves in the tourist rough-and-tumble that is Venice in early September, and asked to speak to the superintendent. When our turn to be served came, I flourished my papers – very important in Italy! – and we were dealt with swiftly and amicably. Foreigners who reside in Italy or who own a business there require both a *permesso di soggiorno* and a *carta di soggiorno,* and they have, naturally, to present identification. I asked the superintendent to be kind enough to look up Adrian Carrick in his records. What he found was this. *Il Signor* Carrick had owned the Galleria Assunta since 11 September 1970, in partnership with a Swiss citizen, Herr Ueli Fehrmann. He gave his permanent address in the United Kingdom as The Cottage, Little Comberton, Worcestershire, and his place and date of birth as Salisbury, 1 March 1914. It was definitely schoolmaster Carrick. Why was I not convinced?

The only recourse left to me was to ask the immigration superintendent to keep a close watch on the Galleria Assunta. If it reopened or was put up for sale or the insurance was renewed, I wished to be informed immediately. If there was such a person as a schoolmaster-Carrick-double, I reasoned that he could not remain in hiding forever. Sooner or later he would have to realise his assets, and I wished to be there when he did. I also informed the superintendent of our progress in the matter of the death of schoolteacher Carrick and of the continuing threats to Faustina. He knew of international gangs operating in Venice in particular and in Italy in general, although it was not specifically his province. I told him that I was there and then returning to the Venice police to lodge with them the little that we knew, in the hopes that something could be done. Spooner and I, as offshoots of the Worcestershire CID, were in effect powerless in such a situation, and we should do better to leave the matter with the Italian police. He agreed and promised his cooperation if it should be required.

Would you care to read the report I submitted to the DCI at this juncture, on our return to Worcester? You shall.

<u>Adrian Carrick, deceased (10 August 1974)</u>. Sergeant Spooner and I were appointed to the case on 26 August, in the light of testimony provided by a Mr George Bolster of Little Comberton. That same day we had identified the man sighted (by Mr Bolster) walking with Mr Carrick minutes before his death as Johnnie Levers, a well-known member of the criminal classes. Mr Levers had gone to some trouble to cover his tracks, but we are sure that our identification is secure. Unfortunately, he has disappeared. It is urgent, therefore, that he be found, so that we can discover who hired him to kill Mr Carrick.

In the meantime, we prosecuted our inquiries in Italy and Switzerland, having discovered through his son Maurice, who runs an art gallery in Birmingham, that Mr Carrick seemingly led a different and secret life in Venice. We interviewed his business partners in an art venture – an Italian woman called Faustina Scaglia, who shares his Venice flat, and a Swiss art-dealer called Ueli Fehrmann, who lives in Zürich - and were told that Carrick had double-crossed the cartel of which he was a member. It then transpired, however, that this was a different Adrian Carrick altogether: Ms Scaglia took schoolmaster Carrick's death to be a mistake on the part of the assassins, who had really intended to kill art-dealer Carrick; it was only a matter of time, she said, before they realised their mistake and came for the 'real' Adrian Carrick.

If we are to make any progress in the continued absence of Mr Levers, we need to resolve the puzzle of the two Carricks.

1. If, as we were first told (by Ms Scaglia), there are two Adrian Carricks, a schoolmaster and an art-dealer, three possibilities present themselves.

A. Partners, either in the business or in the cartel, concerned to mete out reprisals on art-dealer Carrick (as punishment for a double-cross) deliberately target an innocent England-based homonym in order to frighten art-dealer Carrick. (This possibility does not seem to have occurred to Ms Scaglia.)

B. Alternatively, they make a mistake and kill the wrong Carrick.

C. To escape from his enemies, art-dealer Carrick lays a false trail by putting schoolteacher Carrick out of the way. While those that matter to him think he is dead, he slips through their clutches and re-emerges elsewhere under another name, safe and sound.

On all these suppositions, schoolteacher Carrick is innocent of any criminal activity: a harmless academic used as a pawn in a vicious game of feint and double-feint.

2. If, on the other hand, there is only one Adrian Carrick, as his Italian fancy piece assured us latterly, masquerading alternately as a schoolteacher in England and as an art-dealer in Venice, he was killed for the reason outlined above, namely double-crossing his partners in crime, but it was his own misdeeds that brought the nemesis on him.

However, we have also rehearsed alternative theories, centring variously on Carrick's (= schoolmaster Carrick's!) acquaintance with a school-leaver from Grant College, on his place in the college, and on his private life. We have even considered whether his death might not have been accidental, whether he was killed by someone who thought he knew too much, and whether he was the random victim of a gangland killing. We have interviewed a significant number of people, from his headmistress to a female friend, from the girl on whose account some thought he had committed suicide to several of her male acquaintances. In short, we have cast a wide net. After a week and a half of vigorous activity, however, we have refined but not solved the motive for Adrian Carrick's death. Unless further evidence is forthcoming, it is not easy to see where we can go next. We are limited to awaiting the arrest of the elusive Mr Johnnie Levers, and even that may not be so enlightening as we hope.

'Solving' the crime, by which I mean identifying its principal agent and his or her motive, will do nothing to relieve the grief of Mr Carrick's family, but it could lay to rest once for all any hint of illegality and of double-dealing in his private life; it could, in a word, clear his name and allow his memory to continue unsullied. These are worthy aims, but you must decide, Sir, whether the circumstances warrant our spending more time on the case.

I suppose I hoped that the DCI would allow us to continue, although quite where we went from our present position was unclear. I took some comfort from many previous cases, in which we spent time and energy (and, I fear, pecuniary resources) in amassing large amounts of detail, much of it irrelevant, but emerged victorious at the last because one specific point, the pertinence of which had escaped us at the time, suddenly shone through as the key to the unravelling of the crime. So, for example, in the case of the death of John Goode, it was a throw-away remark on his aunt's part which triggered the solution. In the case of the sad deaths of the elderly Patience and Walter Falshaw, poisoned in their daughter's cottage in her absence, I was put on the trail of the murderer by an unremarkable characteristic of one of the principal characters in the drama. Again, when a valuable mediaeval manuscript caused mayhem round a peaceful monastery in Warwickshire, it was a harmless piece of French ballet music which prompted me to take a new look at the evidence we already had. When Fr Wilfred Tarbuck tumbled out of his confessional, never to stir again, I had the crucial clue to hand almost from the beginning, but I made nothing of it until my wife told me, when already some weeks had passed, about the novel she was reading. In the case of the deaths incident on a theft from a rural school in deepest Worcestershire, in which the Founder's portrait was damaged, my failure to put to one of the actors in the drama a short and simple question prevented us from seeing where the solution lay. I could go on. As I have constantly reminded my sergeants, since it is impossible to distinguish at first what is relevant and what is not, it is essential to amass material widely and carefully, with meticulous records, in the hope that at some point the significant factor will be spotted. It is often tedious work, which sometimes takes the edge off the pleasure of detection, but in my experience success often depends on it. Perhaps I am just an old buffer.

Ten

Then, all of a sudden, four separate events took place in two days, which promised to clarify the mystery of Adrian Carrick's death. Let me tell you about them, in no particular order. They crowded in on us with the urgency of a forest fire and – alas - the ambiguity of La Gioconda.

Firstly, the insalubrious Johnnie Levers was run to earth in a London bed-sit, where he was sheltering from the long arm of the law, or, on an alternative reading, spending a few quiet days in the capital sightseeing. A particularly observant policeman on his beat noticed a dubious character skulking through the streets one night, identified him from 'wanted' posters and made an immediate arrest with the assistance of some support from the station nearby. I was invited to travel up to London to conduct an interview. Spooner accompanied me. Fortunately (I supposed, although this may be malicious prejudice on my part), Mr Levers had been made to shower and change before we were shown into the police cell where he was being kept. He was, as Mr Bolster had testified, short and squat. Heavy features sat under a sloping brow, rather in the manner of *homo australopithecus*, and his unshaven state added to the general appearance of mindless thuggery: not, I wondered idly, a brother of our Bologna barman, by any chance? I opened the batting.

'Mr Levers, we have not met before, but you will have been told who I am and why we – ' as I indicated Spooner ' – are visiting you today. Now, what can you tell us about the murder of Adrian Carrick on Bredon Hill early last month?'

'Nothing.' (I am, by the way, giving you a sanitised and more or less grammatically correct version of our friend's discourse. Otherwise you might be traumatised into abandoning this narrative.)

'This attitude will do you no good in the court, My Friend. It is in your own interest to cooperate,' I said soothingly. After more similar

88

cajoling and sweet-talking, I prevailed so far on Levers as to extract the following account, which I cobble together from his answers to my shrewd and incisive questioning.

'I was minding my own business, as usual,' he said, 'and living my life quietly and wholesomely, when I suddenly thought that the world would like to read my life-story. Here I was, the son of a broken marriage between an alcoholic father addicted to gambling and a consumptive, chain-smoking nymphomaniac mother, expelled from three schools, gang member, recidivist petty criminal, bank-robber; illiterate, unqualified, mindless; when all of a sudden I woke up to life's realities, turned myself around and grew to constructive and exemplary citizenship. But how was I to put this laudable aim of presenting my life-story to an expectant public into practice? How was I to tell the world that it is possible to pull oneself up out of the gutter and become an honest, law-abiding person? I can't write, see. I was mulling over this problem with a few blokes in the pub, when one of them said, "I know, Johnnie," he says, "what you need is a ghost writer." "What's that?" says I. "He's someone what writes your books for you. You tell him what to put down, and he does it." "OK," says I, "I like the idea, but where am I going to find such a person?" "I've got just the bloke in mind," he says, "a schoolteacher, with plenty of time on his hands, like all schoolteachers have: also articulate, generous, interested in bringing the plight of England's poor and downtrodden to a wider audience; just the job." "And where do I find this geezer?" I naturally asks. "Bloke by the name of Carrick; The Cottage, Little Comberton; couldn't be easier. Don't mention my name, though. Let him think you've thought up the idea for yourself: that'll impress him." So one day, when I'm down that way anyway on business, I call in and find him at home. "I was just going out for a stroll," he says, "fancy coming along with me?" So the two of us set off, as amiable as you please, and we get on just fine. He gives himself no airs and seems to take to my idea. We get to the top of Bredon Hill, and I say, "You'll have to excuse me, my way lies down towards Woollas Hall and St Catherine's Farm. Can I call you later?" "That's no trouble," he says, "I'll be happy to go down with you." So we cut down through the woods by St Catherine's Well, chatting away about my book, and him getting all enthusiastic about it and asking me all sorts of questions about me and my life, really sympathetic. Suddenly he says, "Hold on a minute, Johnnie," he says, "just let me check on my large bittercress." "What's that?" I naturally ask. "It's a rare variety of *cardamine amara*. Heaven knows how it got to the bottom of the quarry, but there it is. We don't have to climb down to it: we can view it from the top. A friend told me that this specimen is extremely rare, in fact so rare as to be almost unique to this quarry, and I like to keep an eye on it." At that he leads me off the path to the top of the quarry. "Oh, dear," he suddenly says, "I don't feel so well, I think I'm going to faint." Before I could hold on to him, he'd gone, just like that. Well, was I gobsmacked. He was there one minute, gone the next. Of course, my first thought, as a model citizen, was to summon help. My second thought was, "Hold on a minute: what if someone takes it into his head to accuse me of murder? The world's full of mischief-makers, and I don't want to end up inside again, do I?" So shall I tell you what I did? I legged it as fast as I could, that's what I did. I dropped everything else, hared back to Carrick's place and drove off fast. Why had I borrowed a car through a mate? Why try to cover my tracks? Let me tell you, Inspector: I hadn't got a licence or insurance, and I knew I'd blot my copybook if anything happened and it was found out, so I did my best to be inconspicuous and hide behind someone else's prudence. Why had I gone to London? Because I fancied a few days' quiet sight-seeing. Nothing criminal in that, is there? I had an urge to stroll down Pall Mall and sit in Trafalgar Square watching the world go by. So that's the long and the short of it, Squire, straight up.'

Despite admiring the man for his ingenuity, power of invention and aplomb – how could I not? – I did not believe a word of what he said (and neither do you, I warrant). To quote the monk Glendinning, 'These things, Sir Knight, hang not so well together, that I should receive them as gospel'[4]. However, possible confirmation of his story came later from a curious quarter, as you shall see.

Secondly, we had a fax from the Venetian police to say that a body had been found floating in the lagoon, believed to be that of Adrian Carrick, art-dealer. I had, as I told you, left a request with the *questura* in the Sestiere Santa Croce to be informed of any development in the case, and I was gratified that my confidence was not misplaced. The story was simple. A water-taxi-driver had set out early on Sunday morning from his house at the west end of the Giudecca to pick up a fare at the east end, and he had seen the body floating not far off-

---

[4] Said to Sir Piercie Shafton in Sir Walter Scott's The Monastery, chap. xxvii.

shore. He had informed the police, naturally, and preliminary inspection had shown that the body had been in the water for several days; that death had been caused by strangulation; that papers, notably a very soggy identity card, named him as Adrian Carrick, of Fondamenta Venier. In the absence of traceable next of kin, the *portiere* had identified the body. The file the police drew up, with the assistance of their British colleagues, and extensively edited by me in the light of our later knowledge(!), read as follows:

Adrian Carrick, aka Peter Simpson. Dob 23 September 1916. Place of birth: Redditch, England, second child, second son. Tall (1.82m), slightly built, brown hair, green eyes, no distinguishing marks. Parents: Robert Simpson and Dora Reid, mar. Redditch 4 August 1911. Secondary schooling: Bournville School, Griffins Brook Lane, Birmingham. University: BA in Fine Art at Chester; PhD Studentship Liverpool John Moores. Employment: Faculty Research Manager, Leeds University 1948-52; Deputy Curator, Opera del Duomo, Florence, 1953-61; Acquisitions Director, Accademia di Belle Arti, Florence, 1961-1970. Acquires lease of Galleria Assunta, Calle Selle, Venice, September 1970.

No marriage is known. Adrian Carrick (the name by which he was known in Venice) was a well-read and intelligent student of fine art, with a particular grounding in the Italian *quattrocento* and *cinquecento*, about which he had published two or three papers (under his original name) in scholarly journals (eg 'Gaetano Filippi: artista veneto quattrocentesco ignoto', *Arte e Cultura Veneta* 15 [1965], 19-37; 'La cupola come luogo di culto artistico, Venezia 1200-1500', *Bollettino dell'Accademia Barruti* 21 [1967], 120-129). His managerial skills were well developed, and his employers in Florence were more than satisfied with the discharge of his duties (until the final parting, that is). In character, he was reserved, firm in his opinions, apolitical, a non-practising Anglican (precise religious views unknown), ascetic. Hobbies: none known.

The Italian authorities, concerned for some time that the Galleria Assunta was a front for other, less than legal, activities, had been following his peregrinations and those of his two business partners, a Swiss citizen called Fehrmann and an Italian national known as Faustina Scaglia, but no firm evidence of irregularity was ever adduced. Carrick came and went unpredictably, travelling mainly in western Europe but occasionally to South America. Police experts, in an office sadly undermanned and underfunded, suspected the existence of a cartel, but if there was one, its members were extremely cautious; they also suspected that Carrick was its leading light, but they could never prove it. Quite why Carrick should turn to dishonest activities was not established.

The gallery itself sold a wide range of paintings, including some modern works by present-day artists if they had a Venetian theme, but the emphasis was on Venetian art of the Gothic and Renaissance periods: Gentile, Bellini, Carpaccio, Il Pisanello, Sebastiano del Piombo etc, whose works sold for sums ranging from a few thousand lire to millions of lire. Orlandina and Faustina constituted a discrete and attractive team whose charms were not the smallest attraction of the gallery.

Faustina had been engaged in the very earliest days, when Carrick, realising that he could not both man the gallery and continue his work of acquisition without regularly shutting up the gallery to free him for travel or attendance at local auctions, advertised for a sales assistant with a background in fine art. As the months passed, he realised that Faustina was an asset and that she too could help the business expand if he put in place a subordinate sales assistant: Orlandina. It was at that time that he invited Faustina to move into the flat in the Fondamenta Venier. Since the ladies' combined efforts sufficed to ensure the gallery's financial success, it was more of a puzzle than ever that Carrick should have founded a cartel (if he did).

All this, as you can imagine, set me thinking, and I engaged the services of young Spooner to stimulate my senescent brains.

'Well, Sir,' he said diffidently, 'I can't improve on your own analysis of the role that art-dealer Carrick might have played in schoolteacher Carrick's death.' Toady. 'That is to say, we now know that Venetian Carrick existed and that he was not schoolmaster Carrick in disguise, moonlighting in Continental Europe to eke out his pitiful salary as a chalk-face hack. Let us look at the options facing us!

'Firstly, let us suppose that there is no connection whatever between the bogus Carrick's Venetian activities and the real – schoolmaster - Carrick. His *nom de guerre*, or war-name, to be truer to our noble English tongue, except that no one would know what you were talking about, was fortuitously chosen and indicates no sinister intent. His death is the result of some squabble or disagreement that is no concern of ours, indeed of no interest to us.

'But secondly, what if we posit some connection, denoted perhaps by the deliberate choice of pseudonym on the part of Venetian Carrick, between the two men? Here our options are subtler.' Spooner paused to make a few notes on the pad in front of him, thus (I thought) properly marshalling his thoughts. 'We have four possibilities, each one more confusing than the last.' He sucked the end of his biro, clearly staggered by the complexity of the situation thus disclosed. 'Shall I take them one at a time, Sir?'

'Yes, of course,' I said tartly, 'how else are you going to manage it?'

'Right, for the sake of easy comprehension, I shall label them A to D.'

'Yes, yes,' I said, 'for heaven's sake get on with it, or I shall be obliged to do it myself!'

'Doesn't somebody somewhere, Sir, say that patience is all the passion of great hearts?[5] Sorry, Sir: I'll get straight to the point.

'Option A, then. Let me preface this first option with the remark that I am distinguishing the two Carricks, now that we know for certain that there are two, by calling them VC for Venetian Carrick and PC for Pershore Carrick. VC deliberately targets PC so that if anything goes wrong with his own activities, the latter takes the rap. This idea requires that the Pershore connection is known amongst VC's enemies, whom he must have realised he was making, and to the Italian police. At the first sign of trouble, VC ducks out of sight, and any trail leads inexorably to PC.

'B. The connection between VC and PC is not sought by the former but is an error on his enemies' part, or possibly, as has been suggested to us, on Orlandina's part. VC may not even realise that people are confusing two different men. He is as innocent of deception as the brightness of a new-born day, as Wordsworth nearly said.

'C. Faustina is the agent of the confusion, building on an initial mistake of Orlandina's. In the first instance, she wishes to canvass our

---

5
James Lowell, in his *Columbus*: line 241

help in protecting her beloved VC, until she realises that that is not our prime concern. She then changes her stance to protect him by denying his existence altogether. If we can be persuaded that he doesn't exist - and what might a few fluttering eyelashes and a bit of simpering not achieve in that direction? - we shall go away attributing a double life to PC and forget about VC.

'D. The connection was actually initiated by PC, who suggested it to VC on a visit to Venice, or perhaps before, as a cover for his own illegal activities. If there is a cowboy already on site, so to speak, PC can swan off to Venice and back again, using VC as a cover, and if anything goes wrong, he can point to VC and say, "There's your man, nothing to do with me".

'The question remains, what light can any of these options shed on PC's death on Bredon Hill? Are we any wiser?'

'Yes, Sergeant, I'm agog to hear your conclusions. Your exposition so far is masterly, but be assured I shall say nothing to the DCI about it, in case you are promoted above me. Please carry on.'

'OK, Sir. This is what we get,' again scribbling on his pad. 'On Option A, schoolmaster Carrick is done to death by the same gang as targeted poor art-dealer Carrick. They got the wrong man, realised their mistake, and rectified it, with the results contained in the latest fax from Venice. Here VC carries the weight of responsibility for PC's death, because it was his deliberate confusion which misled his enemies. On Option B, schoolmaster Carrick is the innocent victim of a mistake on the part of VC's enemies; VC is in the clear. On Option C, Faustina built on a mistake of her underling's, realising that she had therein a weapon to protect VC. PC is still an innocent victim, poor man, but in this case the responsibility is Faustina's, and she can still be held responsible for it – if she has survived her employer's murder, of course. On Option D, finally, PC was dabbling where he shouldn't and got more than his fingers burnt. The murderous gang got one over on him. That reminds me of a cartoon I once saw, Sir, if I may interrupt myself for a moment. The picture is of two fencers, one of whom slices the head off his opponent. The caption is simply *"Touché!"* Good, isn't it, Sir?'

'It is, and it reminds of a similar cartoon I saw a long while back. A batsman slices at the ball in a 360º arc and takes the wicket-keeper's head off. The caption is: "Oops!" Sorry, Sergeant, back to the matter in hand – but you started it!'

'Yes, Sir, sorry, Sir. Now if none of these four Venetian options satisfies us, we have to fall back on our very first suggestion, namely, that the solution to Adrian Carrick's murder in Worcestershire has nothing whatever to do with Italy and must be sought elsewhere: presumably in Worcestershire. None of the Italian options is within our remit: we can hardly hot-foot it back to *La Serenissima* to track down and arrest a gang of art thieves – or whoever they are – although possibly the delicious Faustina could be within our grasp. Either course would entail time and effort, and we should probably be better advised -- subject to superior counsel, of course, Sir – to focus on the Worcestershire connection.'

The third event of that momentous day was the report of a break-in at Adrian Carrick's Little Comberton cottage. For those of you unfamiliar with the village, let me describe it briefly so that you have some picture in your mind's eye. Although the church and manor go back to the eleventh century, the present village came into significant existence only in the eighteenth century, and indeed, up until a hundred years ago, consisted of a single street. Nowadays building has created a figure-8 of a village, with the manor-house and the church at the southern tip; a yet further development to the north has added a small enclave on the Wick Road, above the 8. The whole is set in a parish of 800 acres of agricultural land, a patchwork of wheat, barley, orchards and grassland, with tracks and footpaths to indicate where the agricultural workers of old walked out to their day's toil: hedging, ditching, haymaking, pollarding and so forth. Did you know that in September 1826 William Cobbett rode this way? He crossed the Severn at Upton on his route to Worcester, and in his *Rural Rides*, published four years later, he speaks very highly of Bredon Hill – 'one of the very richest spots of England,' he writes – of the local people – 'the working people seem to be better off than in many other parts' – and of the city of Worcester – 'one of cleanest, neatest, and handsomest towns I ever saw: indeed I do not recollect to have seen any one equal to it'. That, however, is a diversion. (I am getting as bad as Spooner.) As the Wick Road leaves the top of the Little Comberton figure-8 behind, travelling north, it cuts through a line of trees which run east and west, and you will then see on your left a short lane – little more than a track, if the truth be told – and there, fifty yards up, you will see Carrick's cottage, snugly set at the edge of a field (laid to hay when we were there). If the village stopped there, it is doubtful whether the milkman and cold-callers would have bothered to visit. The cottage itself, brick under a tiled roof, has already been described: a labourer's homestead, no doubt, once thatched, with a chimney poking out from amongst the reeds and lazy smoke drifting up into the winter air; chickens scratching around in the dirt; an ill-nourished dog sitting on the doorstep and growling in a surly manner at the pecking birds; the only sound the whimper of a cold breeze in the leafless trees, or the creak of the housewife's mangle. I am sorry: I digress - again.

A month had passed since Mr Carrick's fatal fall in the quarry on 10 August. Frances (Haslehurst) and Maurice (Carrick) agreed to meet at The Cottage on the Saturday morning to complete their work of clearing, tidying and sorting, preparatory to the visit of an estate agent to take their instructions. This was not their first visit: they had met there the previous Saturday morning, but on that occasion all was as it should be. Today, however, they found the house in disorder, from top to bottom. Every cupboard and drawer had been emptied and the contents spilt on to the floor; rugs had been pulled up; pictures torn off the walls; papers scattered in bewildering confusion (and, as we knew, in profusion as well). It was, the two said, heartbreaking. The burglar or burglars had helped themselves to food from the kitchen cupboards, leaving half-consumed tins and packets on the work-surfaces and floor. There was little they could do, after making their own selection of a few items by way of souvenir, but make a bonfire of the papers and files, bag up the unusable debris for the dustcart and appoint a house-clearance person to take away the furniture. This, however, was only *after* the police had taken photographs, hunted for finger-prints and looked where they could for clues.

The evidence was wretchedly thin. The burglary could have occurred any time in the previous week and at any time of the day (or night, possibly, but I thought that unlikely, in view of the possibility of lights' being seen from the road); no vehicle need have been involved if the culprit was searching for portable items only, like cash. The burglar had been careful to leave no fingerprints, footprints, teeth-marks or lip-marks; he, or she, or they, had opened drawers from the bottom of chests up - the sign of a professional, I thought. I asked Frances and Maurice whether they knew of any precious item in their father's possession that would have attracted a thief. Frances was too upset to speak, but Maurice said he knew of only a couple of things – an Elizabethan coin their father had once found in a street in Devizes, a couple of rarer Vatican stamps, all kept in a small tin box – and there were a couple of quite expensive (but not rare or ancient) books; but nothing that would have been known to a professional thief or would have made a break-in worthwhile. The tin in question had gone, but that would be true if the burglary had been perpetrated by a passing opportunist.

I asked Spooner for his thoughts on the subject.

'Well, Sir,' he said, 'if the murder had been committed with a view to burglary, why did the thief wait a whole month, or at least three weeks, before going over the house? He would surely have moved in almost immediately, before the family had any chance to remove items of interest. I mean, it's not as if the house were securely guarded or booby-trapped or overlooked twenty-four hours a day by prying neighbours. His best opportunity was in the first days after Carrick's death, it seems to me. There is another objection to the view that the murder was committed with a view to the burglary: the thief could have struck any time during the day in term time, without the need for elaborate schemes involving new cars, brown envelopes and trysts in pubs. If we discount that suggestion, therefore, we could still hold that the burglar committed the murder but then had to wait for the information concerning the item he was after, or that he heard about the valuable item only when the summer holidays had already started. Neither seems very likely to me. We are left, then, with a thief unconnected with the murder. Two possibilities, Sir, as I see it. One, this bloke reads about Carrick's death, does a bit of research, a bit of scouting, perhaps, realises that the cottage lies empty and takes his chance. Two, an idle chap, chancing to pass that way, sees an isolated cottage, knocks at the door to ask for a drink of water or for directions or for what have you, gets no answer, goes round the back and does the place over. In which case we probably haven't a hope of catching him, unless he does other jobs in the district or makes a stupid mistake, like offering a stolen watch cheap to a passing policeman.'

'I concur with your analysis, Sergeant. The upshot is that the burglary is really no immediate use to us: distressing to the family, an affront to Mr Carrick's memory, but irrelevant to the inquiry into his murder. Oh, dear, how depressing it all is.'

Eleven

The fourth event in our group was a letter from Geela, posted in Switzerland three days beforehand. It ran to a large number of pages in a neat hand, with some corrections or changes of thought, and was signed, I thought rather touchingly, 'Love, Geela'. Since I do not consider it to have been a private letter, I feel entitled to let you read it in its entirety – you will have to trust me that I have omitted nothing! – but I have taken the liberty of correcting one or two spelling errors and grammatical slips: I hope you do not mind. Otherwise you get Geela in the raw.

Dear Inspector Wickford (I read: *sic*!)

I hope you don't mind my writing to you, but I feel we have established some sort of rapport and that I can talk to you freely. The truth is, I'm homesick! The reason for that is mainly that *Monsieur le Duc* has arrived at the château for his summer break, and he's making life impossible for everyone: he's domineering, moody, sarcastic, ugly, and I loathe him! I don't have much to do with him, except at lunch, but the whole atmosphere in the house has changed for the worse. Still, he's here only for a fortnight, and then we shall be back to normal (I think). I have another reason for writing to you, and that is to tell you something I'm not sure I mentioned before. It may not be important, and you may know it already from others, although I doubt it, but just in case you don't ... it might have a bearing on Mr Carrick's death. Have you a minute to bear with my ramblings, while I flip back to my school-days – how distant they seem already, and I've not been out of the place two months! – and to the philosophy course in particular? I assure you it's relevant (just!). (Surely I shouldn't be so nostalgic at my age? Goodness me: what shall I be like in sixty years' time? On the other hand, as I say, the circumstances are a little special, and I feel that rambling on will help my mood to lift. You are a patient listener who will sit there as I blather on, and I think I know you well enough to be able to say that. Thank you in advance.)

First of all, how do I spend my days here? My main responsibility is to look after the two children, a boy of seven called Honoré and a girl of five called – wait for it! – Océane. Not bad kids: pretty well behaved, not too snobby, and their English is coming on nicely. If their governesses and au pairs have all been English, they've done a good job. So I get 'em up in the morning, see that they're properly dressed and then take 'em down to breakfast. Breakfast is an informal meal, and members of the household come and go as they wish. Food is put out on a handsome Henri II *buffet*, and one helps oneself. Then the children are allowed a bit of free time, before there are two half-hour lessons in English conversation. The duchess is very keen for the children to grow up fluent in English, even before they know much grammar. Then we go for a walk, perhaps in one of the many parks of the city, or along the quais, or along the Route de Lausanne to enjoy the lake. We have to be back for lunch, for that is the main meal of the day, with the household – and that includes me! - formally seated and flunkeys in evidence to serve. It's all a bit daunting when *M. le Duc* is in residence, but the duchess herself is much more relaxed. There are usually family members – uncles, aunts, cousins, what have you – and nearly always guests, so that the party consists of anything between four and fifteen people. The children don't seem to mind the formality: they've been brought up to it, I suppose.

After a sort of siesta, when the *château* falls quiet and no disturbance is allowed, the children go to a music lesson or music practice, Honoré on the piano, Océane on recorder. Then there is story-telling in English: sometimes I read to them, sometimes I invent something. We then stroll in the gardens or take another short walk or go off to visit little friends.

Occasionally I am told to drive the children out for a bit of sight-seeing, and I'm given money to buy them – and myself! - a treat. Supper comes round eventually: an informal meal, but with as much on the *buffet* as you could wish. I put the children to bed not long after supper, and then my evening is free. I can join the duchess and her guests in the *salon* if I wish, or at a game of *pétanque* in the garden or at a musical evening in the *orangerie*. It's all very civilised, Inspector: but it's not home!

Shall I tell you about the house? Just a few words? It's quite grand, but it's not all that comfortable, really. The floors are generally wooden, without any sort of rug on top, which to my way of thinking makes everything rather cold. Many of the rooms are permanently shut up. The furniture is grand and pretty, but not really *cosy*: there are no chairs which make you feel like saying to yourself, Ooh, wow, I'd like to sink into *that* with a good book. There's quite a lot of the house, and there's a good-sized garden, but it is all rather in the *middle* of things: not like a shooting-lodge at the head of a Scottish glen!

It is an experience, however, and I am very glad to have the chance. My French is improving, partly because I speak to the servants, the children (mostly) and the duchess in French, partly because I study by myself in the evenings. I take the previous day's newspaper, read a paragraph, marking with highlighter pen all the words I don't know, look the words up in the dictionary and try to lodge them in my memory. The next day I go back and rap myself over the knuckles for every word I can't remember! You see, I'm doing my best! The original plan was for me to do three months, but I may have the option of extending that time if I wish; but quite what I'd do all day when the children are at school I'm not sure. In any case, we'd be back in France by then with the duke in residence – and I like Geneva without him!

So to school. Did I enjoy Grant? Yes, I did, all five years of it, with reservations. (I didn't join the school until the second year of secondary education.) The ethos was a little severe, or do I mean straight-laced? It was as if we were all sex-crazed maniacs who couldn't wait to get pregnant. Our freedom was sometimes so restricted you felt like screaming. I mean, looking back, I know the school had to err on the side of caution, partly because the parents expected it, partly because a scandal would have done the place an enormous amount of damage, but honestly! We had no sex education: too dangerous! Or perhaps there was no one on the staff sufficiently unbuttoned to undertake it. So sometimes it felt like being locked in a darkened room, starved of stimulation as well as of information. One thing I think the school did well – well, several things, actually. Because classes and houses were small, you felt known, understood and important: you mattered! And staff took infinite pains with slower pupils; but a lot of things were just too boring for words – but then I suppose you get those things at any school. It's the price you have to pay for being an adolescent (or as my little charges call them, *des ados*!).

Food? OK, I suppose. Chapel? There wasn't *too* much of it, but I can't say it enthused me overly. The staff? Not a bad lot: a few wimps, and one or two grotesque oddities over the years, but competent and pleasant on the whole. The headmistress? Fair, well-meaning, efficient; the parents liked her, and that, I suppose, is the main thing: it ensured bums on seats. The school aimed at, and in my view achieved, a relaxed, purposeful ethos which contributed to a wide education – with the reservations mentioned above. I consider myself well-educated – so far! Am I going on a bit! Just one more short paragraph, then.

Is schooling the best form of education? Isn't single-sex education artificial? Even if school is the best form, how should it be organised? I know people have argued over these things and still do, but all I can say is that I enjoyed Grant. No, that's not quite what I want to say. Grant suited me: I learnt – I think I learnt! – because the conditions were relaxed and yet purposeful: no distractions, plenty of time for study, time for fresh air and exercise as well, and a nice bunch of girls. Who can say how I would have performed at a mixed school, at a state school, at a non-denominational school or abroad? Ah, life's ifs!

Definitely time to move on! You know already how much I enjoyed the philosophy. I went for it really as a sort of fill-in in my last two years at school, not because I knew anything much about it. Mr Carrick had written a paragraph on the subject in the Sixth-Form handbook, and I sort of liked what I read. I'd never heard of Plato or Descartes, but I took to the idea of a bit of logic and a dip into questions like how we know things and how we decide what is right and wrong, so I and a few others in my group decided to go for it. Of course, I knew already that I liked Mr Carrick and his democratic, unpretentious teaching methods. I thought I might enjoy the subject, and I did. So did the others, I think; we certainly spent a lot of time discussing amongst ourselves things like, Is there a concept of nothing? or What is a concept? or How do body and mind interact (if they do!)? Of course, the syllabus was designed for people of our age: it dipped into things, gave us a flavour, rather than covering anything in great depth. It wouldn't have satisfied the requirements of a university examiner, but it was quite good enough in its way. That's my view, anyway.

Now sometimes the sessions were rather intense. We'd be reading a text or working through an exercise or discussing some tricky question – like what is real? or what do we mean by meaning? - and after three-quarters of an hour, you'd had enough, particularly at the end of a longish day. Mr Carrick detected the mood of the class very quickly, and he'd close that down and move on to something a bit lighter to fill in the last quarter of an hour or ten minutes. That's how we came to be discussing death: more than once! (Something lighter, did I say?) It was obviously a topic he thought important, even though it wasn't on the syllabus.

He'd start by telling us about, say, Demosthenes, the fourth-century orator. Demosthenes spoke out vigorously against the pretensions of the Macedonian Philip and had eventually to flee to safety. He found refuge on the island of Calauria, just off the coast of the Peloponnese – I think it's spelt Kalaureia, or something like that, today - and sought asylum in the temple of Poseidon. Knowing that this was the end, he sucked poison from the hollow of his quill and then penned the following words: 'I leave you, great god Poseidon: the Macedonians have not left even this sanctuary unsullied'. Mr Carrick'd then ask us for our reactions, gently probing so that we might all have a chance to speak if we wished or stay silent if we preferred. Or he'd tell us about Socrates. According to Plato, in the *Phaedo*, Socrates was cheerful in the face of death: "he did not shake or change his expression but prayed to the gods that his passage to the next world might be a happy one". His last words, as reported by Plato, were, if I remember rightly, "We owe Asclepius a cock, Crito; please don't forget to pay this debt," and with that he was gone. Then, after a suitably solemn pause, Mr C would ask us quietly whether this was a heroic death or whether Socrates should perhaps have defended himself more vigorously against those who accused him, so that we didn't get the impression that he was guilty as charged. (I have just finished reading *The Exploits of Brigadier Gerard*. I wonder what Mr C would have made of Gerard's comment on the death of the traitor Colonel Montluc: 'He had lived hard, this Montluc, and I will do him justice to say that he died hard also'!)

On one occasion he – I mean Mr C, not Socrates! - broadened the subject by telling us that the thoughts of the ancients, particularly of Plato, Seneca and Horace, but also of the philosopher-emperor Marcus Aurelius, had been very influential in shaping the thoughts of medieval Christianity on this matter. I suppose death was much more vivid to the ancients and to the mediaevals than it is to us today: we've airbrushed death out of society by relegating it to professionals and sweeping it into a corner of our unconscious with our modern medicine and extended life-expectancy. So pre-Christian Greek philosophy moulded the way medieval Christians thought about death, and that has percolated through to modern times. Should we bother to think about death at all? After all, there's very little we can do about it. Well, the present-day German philosopher, Heidegger – I think he calls himself an ontologist: a student of being – who is an atheist, has said that it is only by taking death on board that we can come to analyse and assess life properly. According to Mr C, Plato said much the same thing. So we should consider the difference between death and dying, the nature of death – is it something to be welcomed or deplored? for example – what philosophers have said about death from their own perspective, whether and how we can prepare for death, whose deaths can act as models for us, and so forth. According to Heidegger – or perhaps I'm mixing him up with someone else here – death is the one moment in life (so to speak!) when the way we dispose of ourselves is not reversible. Any other decision we take we can go back on or regret, but death is unalterable. We might as well try to formulate our decision beforehand so that the way we marshal ourselves at the end is what we really want. I'm probably not expressing myself very clearly; perhaps I haven't fully absorbed what Mr C was saying, but I'm only trying to give you a flavour of how Mr C got us thinking, whether we adopted the same perspective as him or not.

Anyway, that was that, but when I heard about Mr C's death in the quarry, it brought these conversations back, and I began to wonder how Mr C himself had faced death. If it was suicide, as we all thought at first, did he go into it with his eyes wide open or was he hustled into a decision by forces too powerful for him to control? Did he welcome death or fear it? These were very disturbing thoughts, but I told myself, Come on, Geela, you're a woman now and mustn't shirk the harder tasks of life. Then you told me, Inspector, at that first meeting of ours, that you were treating Mr C's death as murder. I must say, that was a great weight off my mind, even though, as I told you then, I didn't see how I could be in any way responsible for his suicide. Now murder puts a different complexion on things! Probably it catches you unawares. How did it catch Mr C? Well, my impression was that, of all the people I've met, he was most actively conscious of the need to prepare oneself for death, so, whatever the circumstances of his death, he would be ready: poised, so to speak, to commit his life for evermore – at the moment of truth, as somebody has called death. So I didn't worry too much about death catching him unawares. And then I remembered something he said casually, an aside, if you like, but I can't remember whether I was alone with him at the end of a class when he said it or whether some of the other girls were still around. They might still remember if you can find out

who they were! I'm sorry, Inspector: it's taken me all my time
to get to this point, and I've made you sit through all my
rambling on about this, that and t'other. He was just saying that
his father-in-law had suffered a number of blackouts in recent
months, which were naturally rather disturbing. I forget now
how old his father-in-law is or was, but it doesn't matter. His
father-in-law had consulted a doctor, naturally, and had been
referred to a specialist, but the results of tests were not
conclusive. So the poor man was faced with an unknown
condition which could be permanent or temporary, serious or
minor. (Can one ever call blackouts minor?) He could be doing
something relatively innocuous, like driving or climbing a
ladder or walking by the seaside or a river, and poof! all of a
sudden he's had a blackout and rendered the circumstances
fatal. Not nice. Actually, I don't think Mr C went into all this
detail: I think it's me meandering.

You see, Inspector, I'm sitting in my room, late at night, with
the window open and moonlight streaming in. The house is
very quiet: perhaps most people have gone to bed. I would
have gone to bed myself, but as I told you, I was feeling rather
low this evening and decided to stay up and write to you
instead! Don't you feel honoured? Well, all this reminiscing has
put me into a reflective mood, so I think I'm thinking aloud on
my own account as well as reminiscing about Mr C! However,
to the point. After this preamble about his father-in-law, Mr C
went on to say that he had had two similar blackouts himself in
recent months. He said it concentrated his mind wonderfully!
On the first occasion, he had fallen in the garden and done
himself no harm. On the second occasion, he was wheeling his
bike out of his drive when he sort of collapsed and fell on to his
bike: no broken bones, but quite a few bruises and scratches.
He hadn't yet been to a doctor, partly because he was afraid to
do so, partly because he didn't think the matter was sufficiently
grave to bother the doctor with. Now it's taken me quite a bit of
time to write all this down for you, but if you tell yourself that
most of it is me romancing, you will appreciate that Mr C's
comments were over in seconds: a sort of mumble on the side.
But I have been thinking this evening: what if Mr C, on his walk
on Bredon Hill, felt faint when he was walking near the quarry

and simply tumbled in? It would have been an unfortunate accident, wouldn't it? Nobody's fault, just one of those things.

Anyway – sorry, I keep using that word, don't I? – as I say, this memory has only just come back to me – the memory of Mr C's comments about his blackouts, I mean – and I thought you'd like to know. It might be of no interest at all, and even if it's interesting it might not be relevant, but I'm glad I've taken the trouble to put it down on paper, because it's given me the chance to rattle on about school and philosophy! Thank you so much for putting up with the rest of this letter, Inspector. I'm ready for sleep now, and I bet you are, too!

Love
Geela

PS Wouldn't it be nice if we could meet again some time?

Well, Long-suffering Reader, whatever *you* think, I was flattered to receive this letter, even though I know it was written to relieve the writer's feelings and not to entertain *me*! I thought she wrote a good letter: well-structured, chatty, informative, and I'm sorry I've thrown it away now. (One can't keep everything, you know.) As regards the last bit, I imagine that the same thought that went through my mind went through yours: could it be, could it possibly be, that the thin tale spun by the egregious Mr Johnnie Levers was true after all – or at least substantially true? More curious things than that are known to history!

Twelve

At a further conference, Spooner and I decided (or rather, I decided) that four lines of thought arose from our consideration of the case: not necessarily directly from the latest developments, but from the wider view that they prompted. *Cherchons la femme*, to borrow a phrase of Dumas'. The only woman we had looked at when canvassing possible motives of jealousy was Mrs Phyllida Cruickshank, because she was named in the will: could we have overlooked another? The Italian connection niggled: further talk with Faustina was called for. Then, we had not yet interviewed Adrian Carrick's brother, and that required our attention. Finally, if the burglary at Carrick's house was not the work of an opportunist thief, it could provide enlightenment. At the very least, we needed to give it further thought.

To Spooner fell the task of hunting down another woman, if there was one, in the life of Adrian Carrick, schoolmaster of Little Comberton. This is his report, in full.

I decided – he writes - that the best starting point was Mr Carrick's children, and with this in mind, I gave Maurice Carrick a ring at his Birmingham gallery. He opined that we were barking up the wrong tree, but after a little thought he gave me the name of Joyce Barlow. He could not tell me much about her, but his father had, in his hearing, mentioned her several times, although in what connection he could not recall: possibly making music. He could not remember where she lived, if indeed he ever knew, but he guessed, on unspecified grounds, that she was local – to Pershore, that is. It did not take me long to find a widow Barlow in Pershore, and I went along to see her. She lives in Paddock Close, one arm of which is a row of eight modern detached houses with gardens of diminishing size at the back and spaces at the front large enough for several cars. As a result of my forethought and a telephone-call, she was expecting me but appeared to me to be a little tense: perhaps smart and dynamic young policemen have this effect even on citizens of unimpeachable innocence. I was shown into a neat living-room and offered refreshment, which I accepted. (There is no objection to that, I hope, Sir: I take my lead from my superior officer.) Mrs Barlow is a well-built lady of sixty (I estimate), showily dressed, with abundant greying hair piled on top of her head and held in place with a fetching tortoise-shell comb set with brilliants of some kind: probably glass. A slightly fleshy face set off a pair of brilliant black eyes, and a few choice pieces of jewellery completed the picture of one trying to look her best. It is flattering to think that she may have had yours truly in mind! I liked the woman: a homely, calming type. I explained the nature of my business, and she nodded, making no comment. I asked her first of all to explain how she and Carrick had met.

'When Adrian's wife died,' she said, 'about four years ago, he advertised in the *Evesham Journal* for an amateur musician who might care to join him in a bit of music every so often. Now I play the clarinet – not well, but my sight-reading's good: if I can play it, I can sight-read it – and we got together for a preliminary session. He had some music, I had some music, and we happily bumbled our way through quite a lot of reasonable repertoire. You know the sort of thing: Schumann, Finzi, a bit of Acker Bilk, some reduced Mozart and so on. As we seemed to get on, we both invested in second-hand stuff, and we ended up with quite a stock of sheet-music, and from playing once a month, we got to playing once a week.'

'Did you meet here or at his house?' I asked.

'Always at his house. There were two reasons for that, Sergeant. Firstly, it's easier for me to get around with my car, particularly in bad weather, but the main reason is that I've got no piano. His upright is no Steinway, but it's melodious enough.'

I told her that we were treating Mr Carrick's death as murder, but she had clearly heard that already, I imagine because we had been investigating for several weeks and had interviewed widely. I asked her whether she had any ideas on the subject.

'Well, Sergeant, it's not as if I haven't thought about it. I was fond of Adrian, you know, and it's hateful to think someone might have wished him harm; but no, I haven't come up with anything sensible.'

'I hope you don't mind my asking, Mrs Barlow, but how close were you and Mr Carrick?'

'How close, Sergeant? What are you getting at?'

'Please don't take offence, Mrs Barlow. You must understand that in a case which isn't at all straightforward, we need to explore every avenue. It has occurred to us that someone may have borne a grudge against Mr Carrick, perhaps for placing his affections in an unpopular direction.'

'Yes, I see: I'm sorry if I seemed a trifle sensitive: I'm still coming to terms with Adrian's death. It has hit me hard, as you can imagine. Well, how to answer your question? I think I was getting emotionally attached to him. Eventually, who knows, we might have made a go of things, but we never discussed it. Let me explain something to you, Sergeant, because as yet, I imagine, you have no experience of widowerhood. Am I right?'

'Quite right, Mrs Barlow.'

'It takes years – probably a lifetime – to overcome the grief of bereavement, but unfortunately one's affections and emotions don't stay put to allow breathing-space. One has social and personal needs that, if unfulfilled, leave one unhappy, lonely. So when a widower and a widow meet frequently, as in our case, the relationship must go forwards or backwards: it can't stay still, that's just not the way of it. It was the music that kept us meeting, week after week, but it was inevitable that emotion began to overlie the social occasion. I think I can say without false modesty that Adrian saw in me someone he could rely on and warm to and generally get on with.'

'And what about you, Mrs Barlow?'

'I was happy to continue as we were, knowing that it can be fatal to hurry in these circumstances. I was very fond of him. In love with him? I really don't know, Sergeant.'

'How many people knew about your weekly sessions?'

'Lots, I imagine. There was no secret about it. My friends knew: I presume his did as well.'

'Do you have children, Mrs Barlow?'

'Yes, two boys.'

'How would they react to your remarriage?'

'How should they react? They're both sensible enough, I believe, to allow me to lead my own life.'

'But – I'm sorry, Mrs Barlow, it's one of the questions I have to ask: pure routine, you understand – your remarriage would effectively disinherit your sons.'

'You're romancing, Sergeant, if I may say so,' and she turned noticeably cooler towards me. 'Neither of my sons would object to my remarriage on those grounds. They're both well off, they want the best for me: mercenary considerations like those you hint at would be anathema to them. In any case, I had never mentioned to them any possibility that Adrian and I might one day marry. It was just never a topic of conversation, whatever they may have thought.'

I left Mrs Barlow with questions seething in my mind: was she accurate in her assessment of her sons' desire to leave her free to lead her own life and remarry unopposed, if that is what she wished? By the same token, was Maurice Carrick's lack of familiarity with Mrs Barlow feigned? Did he and/or Frances resent the idea that their father might remarry? Against that was the fact(?) that there had been no talk of remarriage on their father's part either with Phyllida Cruickshank or with Joyce Barlow. To murder their own father would have been seriously pre-emptive. The unworthy thought also occurred to me that perhaps Joyce Barlow was the culprit: rebuffed by Carrick, she plotted and exacted revenge, but perhaps I was being fanciful.

Here endeth the first report.

Thus far Spooner on Mrs Barlow. His report left me troubled: we seemed to be flailing at every turn. It is at this stage in an investigation that I contemplate early retirement.

It also fell to Spooner's lot – while I was ensconced in Venice with the divine Faustina, about which you shall hear shortly – to interview

Adrian Carrick's brother Winslow. Again, here is his report in full.

Judith and Winslow Carrick live in a detached house on the corner of Woodlands Road and Church Lane in the village of Mildenhall (also known as Minal, I was told), just to the east of Marlborough: lovely Wiltshire countryside, but just a bit too close to the A4 for comfort – in my opinion! The house has a large garden with a tennis-court, a pond, a small orchard etc: whatever Mr Carrick's job (I discovered later that he had been in marine insurance), it clearly pays better than his brother's! It was early evening by the time I had covered the sixty miles from Worcester, and I was invited to join them in an aperitif (I settled for a fruit juice). Winslow Carrick is quite dissimilar to his brother in build (if I have a right picture of Adrian in my mind): a much solider, heavier figure, with plump features and an unhealthy hue – the result, I presumed, of excessive indulgence in the fruits of the hop and the vine and inadequate exercise! His wife is petite and quiet: I put her down as a home-maker rather than as a career-woman. After introductory pleasantries and my commiserations on their bereavement, I had to explain that we were working simultaneously on two main lines of inquiry: the death was an accident, the death was murder. The latter was not a surprise, since they had had occasion to contact Winslow's nephew on their return home – and they had been told about the burglary - but the former *was*.

'But we thought the coroner's verdict quite clear, Sergeant.'

'It was, Sir, but a considerable amount of new evidence has since come to light.'

I proceeded to fill them in on that part of our investigation, paying particular attention to the supposed assassin and his version of events and to Geela's revelation about Adrian's blackouts. I asked Winslow what he thought.

'No, it's news to me, Sergeant: first I've heard about blackouts. As far as I knew, Adrian was fit in every respect.'

'May I ask, Sir, how much of Adrian you had seen in the past few years?'

'Yes, you may ask, and the answer is, as you seem to be implying, not very much. The situation is this. I am eight years

Adrian's senior: there was a sister born between us, but she died years ago, I regret to say. Adrian and I had therefore never been what you might call close: when I went up to university, Adrian hadn't even started secondary school. After school Adrian went off to Oxford, then eventually Leeds, then to his first teaching post in Exeter, whereas I spent most of my working life in London, and we met only occasionally: family baptisms, weddings and funerals, that sort of thing.'

'We have not been able positively to exclude a connection between your brother and a firm of art-dealers in Venice. Might you know anything about that?'

'No, but what can that have to do with his death?'

I outlined the results of our trips to Venice, and he was astonished that such a thought as a double life for Adrian could ever have occurred to us.

'No, no, Sergeant, for goodness' sake, Adrian wasn't that kind of person at all: he had integrity. I'd say "simplicity", but that might give the wrong impression. No, you can discount that entirely.'

'But, Sir,' I persisted, 'if your brother kept his Italian activities concealed even from his own children, is it surprising that he didn't parade them round the rest of the family?'

'I tell you, Sergeant,' Carrick said, a little impatiently, I thought, 'such a double life as you imply would be quite out of character. Adrian was devout, serious, straightforward. Wheeling and dealing, duplicity and such-like would be totally foreign to him. He used often to quote Milton at me: "No falsehood can endure Touch of celestial temper," whatever he meant by that, exactly.'

'Right, Sir, that is well noted. Can we move on to possible motives for murder? I know it can't be very pleasant to think of a close relative's being the victim of a hired killer, but if matters did develop in that direction, would you have any ideas?'

'No, none, Sergeant. In my view, Adrian was as harmless an individual as you would encounter on a day's march.'

'Well, let me fill you in on the angles that have so far occurred to us. One, your brother owned something valuable but had to be removed before his house could be properly searched for it.

Two, he was the victim of a woman who had rebuffed him or of a woman who resented his attentions to someone else. Three, somebody realised that his remarriage would effectively disinherit him or her.'

'You mean Frances and Maurice?' Carrick said disbelievingly.

'No, Sir, not necessarily: could be the children of the woman he married. Shall I go on? Four, an Italian gang used him to frighten another man of the same name into compliance. And there are one or two other ideas, but as they seem less likely, I shall spare you the details.'

'As what, for example?'

'Well, we have considered the possibility that someone – perhaps boyfriends of Geela Purdew - resented his friendship with her, even though we consider it to have been entirely proper. Or there is a remote possibility that he had heard or seen something to somebody else's disadvantage and had to be killed as a possible witness.'

'Yes, I see, Sergeant,' Carrick said in a more conciliatory tone. 'I can see that it's not been entirely straightforward for you.'

'Well, that's precisely our problem: because your brother seems to have been so upright and simple in his tastes and activities, it is very difficult to see why anyone should wish to get rid of him. In the light of all this, may I ask you again whether anything comes to mind, anything at all?'

Carrick sat there for a moment. Eventually he spoke.

'There was an incident a few years ago,' he said slowly, 'but I just can't see it having any bearing on our present subject. It seems so trivial.'

'Please go on, Sir,' I said encouragingly.

'Adrian was in a sense self-contained, by nature placid and not easily ruffled, although that was merely the exterior of a complex, rich and sometimes restless personality. In the days of which I am talking now, he wore a moustache in the handlebar style – a bit affected in my view, but presumably he had his reasons. One evening there was some do on at school, Adrian attended, and the atmosphere was relaxed. One of the younger girls expressed her intention of stroking his moustache, and he advised her against it. She persisted and was again warned. In the end she put her hand up with a sudden movement and tweaked one end of his moustache. Adrian did not lose his temper, but he was affronted and disappointed that the girl could not see he was serious; he slapped her lightly on the cheek. This almost trivial gesture was noticed by another member of staff who thought it her duty to bring it to the head teacher's notice. The parents were informed and created merry hell. Eventually the incident was smoothed over, but it left a mark on Adrian's bonhomie. One minor result was that he shaved the moustache off. As I say, Sergeant, I'm not quite sure why I'm telling you this, because the affair was so slight as hardly to warrant mention, but since that's the only possible thing I can think of, I do mention it.'

'Thank you, Sir, that might be helpful. Do you know the girl's name?'

'No, but the headmistress will know – or can look it up. It's probably gone into Adrian's file, heaven help us.'

Well, since there seemed nothing more to be gained from prolonging the conversation, I came away. I did, however, give the headmistress a ring, and she told me, after consulting the files, that the girl's name was Jacqueline Minscath and that the parents live – or at least lived – in Worcester.

Here endeth the second report.

I pondered these words and came to the conclusion that the incident was unimportant but that we could not afford to neglect it.

On the third matter, that of the burglary at Carrick's house, Spooner and I put our heads together and thought out loud – over a pot of tea, of course.

'Well,' I began in time-honoured style, 'Carrick's children know of nothing valuable in the house. Further, the will makes no mention of any property in particular. We have ourselves gone over the house, not thoroughly, perhaps, but pretty well, and nothing exactly hit us between the eyes. Your thoughts, please, Sergeant.'

'Right, Sir, here's a few at random,' he replied, reaching for his notebook. 'On one hypothesis, the burglar had some particular item in mind. First of all, he did not know where to look: whatever was the object of his search could have been anywhere in the house, as far as he was concerned. Secondly, because he ransacked even small places like drawers, it can't have been a picture, a piece of furniture or an *objet d'art* like a vase or ornament. Thirdly, because he – or she, of course – riffled through papers, what he or she was looking for was not something solid like a diamond or a piece of jewellery. That seems to leave us with a document of some kind: a bill of sale, perhaps, an IOU, a receipt, a sheet of particular postage stamps, or a compromising letter: the possibilities are endless. In other words, the item was possibly not valuable in itself: it had value to someone for reasons other than its intrinsic worth.'

'Yes, good,' I said, 'but that still leaves a whole host of questions, even if we could come to even a tentative conclusion about the nature of what the burglar was looking for. For example, did Carrick know he had it? Why did the burglar wait three weeks before making his attempt? Did he get what he wanted, or is it still hidden in the house somewhere? Or perhaps not hidden, perhaps openly on display if the burglar didn't quite know what he was looking for? And finally, if the burglary and the murder are connected, whatever the sought item was or is must have been of considerable worth to someone. What would be so valuable to you, Sergeant, that you would kill for it?' I left this question hanging in the air, as the answer must surely – surely! – be 'Nothing'. 'Would you like to go on, Sergeant?' I said generously, as I poured myself another cup of life-giving tea.

'OK, Sir, let's think about your questions. Whether Carrick knew he had the item or not is not, with respect, going to help, as it can't shed any light on our investigation – '

' – unless knowledge made him hide it very carefully,' I said.

'There is that, I suppose, Sir,' Spooner conceded, a bit grudgingly (I thought). 'As regards your second question, we can at least hazard a few suggestions, I think. The murderer plans his murder: he hires a professional killer, and that takes time and money; it was not a deed perpetrated on the spur of the moment or on a whim. On the supposition that this is to get Carrick out of the way in order to leave his place free for a going-over, a delay was caused by the murderer's sudden indisposition. Or we can be more subtle than that.' Spooner

115

was getting into his stride: I knew the signs – an acceleration in speech, a forward protrusion of the head, agitated movements of the hands. 'Let us presume that the murder was carried out because an opportunity presented itself, even though the principal was not quite ready for his burglary. For example, the hired killer had only a small window of action, because he had so much else on his plate – a whole string of assassinations in different parts of the country - or the principal thought that Carrick would be shortly on his guard if something came to his attention, for example in a newspaper, or he determined to be more precise about the what or the where than he was. There would be no danger of the house being cleared for some weeks after Carrick's death: these things take time to organise, particularly if the family are not on the spot. Or here's another thought: perhaps the murderer, determined to mystify the dim-witted coppers, deliberately left a three-week gap to make any connection with the murder doubtful, or at least questionable. My conclusion is that, although the delay between murder and burglary is a little bit puzzling, it could have a rational explanation: that's the point I'm trying to make, Sir.' He paused to refill his cup. 'And so to your last questions, Sir, which we can deal with together: did the burglar find what he wanted? There, I think your guess is as good as mine!'

'And we're still not entirely sure that we're dealing with a murder! If Carrick's death was an accident, the burglary could be random. The bloke was looking for cash, or a cheque-book, or a passport, or anything else he could lay his hands on that he could turn to his advantage. Ah, me, what a muddle!' I concluded with a sigh.

Thirteen

Now is the time to tell you about my visit to Venice – the third in less than three weeks – undertaken while Spooner was gadding about the English countryside interviewing upright and harmless citizens (as it seemed). As the plane cruised over the Alps, I reviewed my conversations with Faustina. On my first visit to Venice, on 27 August, the day after Maurice had disclosed the Italian connection, I had eventually run her to ground in a seedy bar in late-night Bologna. In the course of that conversation, she had revealed that she cared nothing for schoolmaster Carrick: all her concern was for art-dealer Carrick, her partner, who was in hiding from his enemies – as indeed was she. She had been swathed in scarves against recognition by her enemies. On the only occasion when her 'disguise' slipped, it was still too dark for me to see her face clearly. On my second visit, on 4 September, during which I was accompanied by Spooner as we had reason to believe we were facing an aggressive and dangerous criminal, we were admitted to her rooms. She had confessed freely, during that second conversation, that she had misled us: there was only one Adrian Carrick, schoolmaster and art-dealer rolled into one, and he was dead. She herself was remaining in hiding until she received word from the cartel. On that occasion, Spooner and I had met her in a darkened room. In my imagination, however, I pictured her as a generously proportioned, opulent, Mediterranean woman still in the fullness of her physical prime, with lush, dark hair, skin a shade of bronze to match her rich, auburn voice and the figure of an hour-glass. It was, on the other hand, quite clear that we could not trust a word she said, although I could add, in her defence and in my liberal interpretation, that her ducking and weaving had been indications, not of an essentially deceptive intention, but of a mistrust of foreign policemen. I wondered how the world had treated Faustina in the week since we had last met.

Uncertain whether to go straight to Bologna or risk a fruitless visit to the Galleria Assunta in Venice first, I opted (in my weakness) for the latter, taking the familiar route from the airport to Mestre and thence to the Grand Canal, where I drew deep breaths to suck in the heady mixture, compounded of sea-water, flotsam, coffee and human perspiration, that is the atmosphere of *La Serenissima* in summer. The city was floating majestically on a calm sea, under a cloudless sky. Water-taxis stood about, waiting for a fare, as the canal lapped gently at the steps that led down from the station. I stood there, gazing across at the worn façade of San Simeon Piccolo and marvelling at the beauty that was Venice. Many of the summer visitors had, I supposed, departed, but the pedestrian traffic in the streets was still brisk – very brisk! There was a lack of constraint and a graciousness in the air that had me wishing for ever longer stays in the city, where some churches boast over a hundred listed works of art, where the art galleries and museums are numbered in dozens, where you can find a concert or recital any night of the year, and where beautiful architecture and intriguing local personages face the visitor at every corner of the street. However, I told myself, to business! Shouldering my light bag, I strolled down the Lista di Spagna, feebly giving in to the temptation of an *espresso* and *dolce* on the way, and approached the Galleria in the Calle Selle somewhat apprehensively. To my satisfaction – and surprise - it was open and functioning. The delightful Orlandina was at her post, and as we chatted, companionably, in the shop, Faustina emerged from the office and advanced to meet me. She was a *little* as I had imagined her: a well-proportioned lady who held herself erect, black hair down to her shoulders, nearer fifty than forty, dressed in dark colours to express (I supposed) her mourning. There was a thin smile of welcome on her lips, although, heaven knows, she had no real reason to expect or desire another visit from me. After thanking Orlandina for her welcome, I followed Faustina into the office and closed the door behind me.

'What can I do for you, Inspector?' she asked.

'Miss Faustina,' I began, 'you have spun me such a rigmarole to date that I no longer know what to believe. Since the discovery of your partner's body last week, I know as well as you do that schoolmaster Carrick was not the same man at all as your partner, but I am still unclear about a possible connection between the two men. I want you now, if you please, to tell me all you know: the truth and nothing but the truth, naked and unvarnished. First of all, please tell me why you have come out of hiding and are openly running the gallery.'

She had the grace, caught in her lies as she was, to look uncomfortable. She took a moment to compose herself – or, as I uncharitably speculated for a moment, to spin a new web of deceit.

'As I told you last time, Inspector, I had instructions to phone the leader of the cartel at a certain time, which I did. He assured me that my time of penance was over, reminded me not to repeat my partner's mistakes, and said that it suited him for the gallery to reopen as soon as possible. So Orlandina and I spent yesterday refreshing our memory of current transactions, catching up on post and preparing the gallery – with dusters and a vacuum-cleaner – for reopening today. It's as simple as that.'

'And how are you feeling in yourself?' I asked kindly.

'Oh, so-so, Inspector. I have thrown myself back into the business, now that I know Peter is dead, and I hope eventually to honour his memory by leading the gallery to ever greater success. But really I'm numb inside and functioning on auto-pilot. Orlandina is very supportive. She's my niece, by the way: you probably didn't realise that.'

'No, I didn't,' I admitted: a veritable family, seemingly, of gorgeous women! 'Please tell me how the gallery started.'

'It all began in Florence,' she said, speaking precisely and in a measured tone, as if to make sure that I understood her perfectly. 'Peter – he adopted Adrian as an alias in Venice – was director of acquisitions at the Accademia di Belle Arti, as you probably know by now. In late 1970, there was, shall we say, a misunderstanding, and Peter thought it best to disappear, adopt a new identity and set up in business on his own somewhere else. As he and I had been living together for some time, I went with him and necessarily changed my name as well.'

What is there about change of name which makes it, for most people, a disturbing experience? A name is an external attachment, chosen more or less arbitrarily and not in any way expressive of personality. Before the Middle Ages – I speak of Europe - people generally had one name only; surnames developed by strange and circuitous routes over several centuries. Forenames are chosen by parents for a variety of reasons, not all of them sophisticated. Yet our name seems to embody our personality: it is who we are. Sorcerers endow the name with particular powers. I have often puzzled over this. If you are interested in these things, Wickfield means '[living in/working on/owning] the field by the dairy-farm or by the hamlet'; and Stanley 'a stoney meadow'! Now I ask you: what does that tell you about me? Nothing whatever! I asked Faustina what her original name was.

'Does it matter? No, it is of no importance now. May I go on?'

I nodded.

'Peter was contemplating how best to go about arranging his change of status. We were in Venice, where he thought we might settle, when he struck up an acquaintance with an English tourist called Adrian Carrick, who seemed keen to cultivate it. Peter made no secret of his desire to adopt a new identity, making out that it would signify his determination to begin a new life. Adrian, whom I met only once, had a wild imagination, and it included ideas really beyond his competence. He made a proposition. Why did Peter not set up a picture gallery, since he had seemingly no little experience in that direction, with Adrian's financial help, and adopt his own name, so that Adrian could dream that he himself was running a successful business in that architectural jewel, *La Serenissima*? This quaint idea appealed to Peter, and, after talking it over with me, Peter decided to go along with it. It would give him a perfectly legitimate second persona and an opportunity to establish a *bona fide* enterprise.' I'll say.

'Sorry to interrupt you there, Faustina,' I said, 'but what did Adrian Carrick get out of the arrangement, apart from delusions of running an art business in Venice?'

'His initial capital input was limited to the establishment of the enterprise: no further funds from him would be required. In return he got a percentage of profits, initially fixed at 10% but reviewable annually. In addition, he had the option to buy any painting in the gallery for what it had cost the gallery to purchase. It was then, while plans were still being laid, that Peter met Ueli Fehrmann, an experienced art-dealer, also interested in setting up a gallery in Venice. He decided to take Fehrmann on board, since the additional capital would enable Peter to specialise in a particular period of Venetian art and acquire specific valuable works to get the ball rolling.'

'Did Adrian Carrick know of Fehrmann's involvement?'

'Possibly not. Does it matter?'

'No, probably not. Please go on.'

'Well, all these initial arrangements suited Peter down to the ground. He now had, not unlimited funds exactly, but certainly ample funds, to set up a gallery, with two partners who would not interfere and would therefore leave him free, but furnishing certain expertise and contacts if required, to manage the business according to his own ideas and experience. With all the paper-work completed – Italian bureaucracy is a bit of a nightmare, Inspector[6] - Peter and I felt secure enough to buy a flat not far from here, and we settled down to our new existence.'

'How did Peter square his new identity with the Italian authorities?'

'He used Adrian's passport to take out new papers, and there was never any suspicion – that I know of – about his new identity. The Venetian authorities were apparently keen to see a new business starting, well-financed and specialising in Venetian art of a certain period.'

'When did things start to go wrong?'

'Well, you know, Inspector, Orlandina and I between us run the business from day to day, and Peter thought he'd stretch his wings by extending his activities, safe in the knowledge that the gallery was satisfying his two partners and that they would not interfere. But yes, after a couple of years, things began to go wrong. Peter got in with a criminal crowd, was persuaded to use his expertise and contacts for nefarious purposes and eventually suffered the final penalty for his greed.'

She sobbed into her handkerchief.

'On the occasion of our first conversation, Faustina, you told me that Orlandina had spotted in a London newspaper news of Carrick's death in Worcestershire, supposedly by suicide. You took that to be a mistake on your enemies' part: a confusion of identities. Do you stand by that interpretation?'

'Peter and I discussed it. Whichever way you looked at it, it seemed to us to be bad news. Either they had genuinely mistaken

---

[6] Will lovers of Italy, and Italian readers of this book, please overlook this comment? JF

schoolmaster Carrick, as you call him, for Peter, or they were firing across Peter's bows by way of warning. Whichever way it was, the message for Peter was clear. The possibility of suicide seemed remote to us, but then we were already nervous and ready to believe the imminence of the slightest threat.'

'And what did you do about it?'

'Peter decided to make an appointment to see – shall we call him Mr Big? – to try to settle the difference between them.'

'And?'

'Well, I don't know any details of the conversation. When he got home, Peter thought he had pacified the boss and that, providing that he, Peter, was guilty of no further slip-ups, all was well between them. He had obviously misunderstood, because a few days later Mr Big sent him a pig's heart. Perhaps he felt that Peter was insufficiently repentant, or perhaps he wanted to make an example of him – a simple Englishman – to keep his other minions in line. That little parcel marked the beginning of the end. Peter immediately said that the two of us must go underground: he didn't want Mr Big to use me to get at him. I ran off to Bologna, as you know, Peter to Padua, where he had friends. We didn't know how long the crisis would last, but we left Orlandina looking after the shop as best she could, with coded ways of keeping in contact. How they got on to Peter I don't know, but the next I knew was that news that his body was found appeared in the press: "Tragic drowning of English art-dealer" etc.' She sobbed quietly into her handkerchief again.

'OK, Faustina,' I continued, after giving her time for an understandable manifestation of her grief, 'but I need to know who this Mr Big is. You see, I'm here to trace Adrian Carrick's killer. Whichever construction you put on it – mistaken identity or warning shot – Mr Big ordered the assassination. He is guilty of murder, no two ways about it, and I need to see that he is brought to justice. Obviously, I'm not going to do that myself, but I need to give the Italian authorities as much information as I can. So what about it?'

She stared at me. 'You can't think of tackling Mr Big? You're mad.'

'No one is above the law, *Signorina*, and this man needs to be tried and convicted. Murder is murder, you know, however important – or more likely self-important – the murderer. Who is he?'

'I cannot tell you. He would know it was me, and then what?'

'Then what? He would be safely behind bars, that's what.'

'I daren't take the risk. There are all his associates; there are Orlandina and my family to consider. No, Inspector, it's out of the question. In any case, what proof have I? None. I guess he sent the pig's heart; I guess he ordered Carrick's murder; I guess he had Peter strangled. But I haven't the slightest proof. How far would you get naming the man to the authorities? Nowhere! and you could seriously jeopardise my own safety and that of my family.'

This lack of proof was a serious setback to my plans, I had to admit. If Faustina could be persuaded to cooperate, some proof might be forthcoming, but I could see that on her present performance nothing was going to be possible.

None the less, I determined to contact the local police. Returning, therefore, to the *questura* in the Sestiere Santa Croce, a fifteen-minute walk away (except that my frequent stops to admire a doorway or a palace façade or a street shrine delayed me), I asked to see the *questore* himself. (The structure of the Italian police forces is of such Byzantine complexity that I should not have known for whom else to ask! I could have been palmed off with any minor functionary.) The quaestor was a man of fifty, with long black hair sleeked back and a nose on which one could have burst a balloon. He seemed cooperative enough. I told him, without concealment, all I knew of Peter Simpson's involvement in illegal activities, all that Faustina had told me about his murder and what I thought about Adrian Carrick's murder; some of this he seemed to remember from my previous visits. I asked whether there was nothing that could be done to apprehend the villains.

'*Signor Ispettore,*' he told me expansively, 'we have had our eye on these people for months, if not years. We know who they are, they know we know who they are, and we know they know we know who they are, and yet so far proof of misdeeds has been impossible to muster, but don't worry: we shall have them eventually, we always do.' He smiled, showing two stark rows of even, yellowed teeth that somehow reminded me of a shark. I was dismissed.

On my way back to the Ponte degli Scalzi, I stopped at a bar on the Calle Lunga delle Chioverette and thought over Faustina's latest revelations. I was sipping a mint syrup (a strong one, at my insistence: left to themselves, bar-tenders stint on the syrup). Faustina wished me to believe that Carrick had gone in with an English stranger whose background he knew to be murky; that he had encouraged him to take on his own name; that for this purpose he had lent him his passport; that he had then had the option of buying in Italian masterpieces at cost price; and all this as part of some wild dream to be dealing in art in Venice. As I looked at this, it came to seem to me less and less credible. All I knew of Carrick spoke against such involvement. Added to this was his children's ignorance of any such activity. On past form, Faustina was an accomplished liar. What could be her purpose in lying to me now? I decided to return to the gallery.

Faustina looked surprised and perturbed to see me, as well she might. I asked to see her in private.

'Faustina,' I said, 'I have returned to tell you that I no longer believe a word you say. I think you are still intent on whitewashing Peter at Carrick's expense. Your story makes out that Carrick initiated the purchase of the gallery and Peter's change of name. That isn't true, is it? You also wish me to believe that Carrick handed his passport over. That isn't true either, is it? This is what really happened. Having escaped from Florence by the skin of your teeth, you and Peter fled to Venice but didn't know what to do next. You saw a hapless British tourist, wandering around on his own looking mournful, and you stole his passport. The details and the photograph were a sufficient match for you to take out residence papers. Carrick knew nothing of all this, beyond the loss of his passport, and he certainly never put money into the venture. I'm right, aren't I?'

She nodded tearfully. I walked straight out of the gallery, too annoyed even to smile at the eye-catching Orlandina hovering in the gallery to inveigle money out of lovers of *cinquecento* Venetian art.

Back in the safety of my Worcester office, I consulted with Spooner and wrote out a report to the DCI. The one firm result of my three visits to Venice, my trip to Switzerland, the search of Simpson's flat, the two clandestine rendez-vous with Faustina (not her real name anyway) in Bologna, the liaising with the Italian police and so forth was that the 'Italian connection' in the case of the death of Adrian Carrick, schoolmaster, was a red herring of enormous proportions. I did not doubt that Carrick had travelled several times a year to Venice, but it was merely as a tourist. I had no idea how long or where he stayed, but it now mattered not at all. His purposes were not in the least sinister. The motive for his death therefore lay firmly in the United Kingdom. Tomahawk had been hired not by some evil Italian crook roosting in Venice and cocking a snook at the forces of law and order but by some unknown English citizen under the noses of the Worcestershire CID. *Ahimé*! It seemed to me in the highest degree improbable that Mr Big had sought out an unknown British schoolmaster for liquidation in the hopes of frightening Peter and Faustina. Apart from any other consideration, he could not be certain that Simpson would ever come to hear of Carrick's death. Furthermore, it would be, and was, reported as suicide, not as murder or criminal assassination. Perhaps I should have picked that up before, I scolded myself. For an experienced and adept detective, I was not doing very well!

Fourteen

Having written a report on my final Venice trip for the DCI's delectation, I was pondering my next move, wondering in particular whether pursuing the incident of the slapped girl would make any kind of sense, when I was jolted out of my indecision by a dramatic development which shaped the rest of the inquiry. I had already more or less decided that the key to the whole affair lay at Grant College, although I should have been hard put to it to give my reasons. Perhaps I relied too heavily on a hunch. On the other hand, we had conducted interviews with the deceased's family (children and brother), his women friends (notably Mrs Phyllida Cruickshank and Mrs Joyce Barlow), his solicitor (Mr Robert Bell), his employer (Mrs Howard) and an unlikely would-be ghost-written autobiographer (Mr Johnnie Levers). There had been an inquest. We had considered the implications of the break-in at his cottage. The idea that Peter Simpson might have been the murderer, which I had mooted what seemed like ages ago, proved unprofitable, as did, indeed, other hypotheses floated in connection with Venice. The possibility that Carrick had been the eye-witness (let us say) of a crime seemed impossible to test. I did not seriously entertain the notion that Carrick had fallen accidentally to his death, although we could not exclude it altogether. All this effort had merely had the effect of narrowing the possibilities down further and further, until the school was virtually the only thing left. We had focussed on Carrick's relationship with the pupils, Geela Purdew in particular: but what of the staff? I decided we had been remiss in this respect and that we should remedy the failure forthwith. I accordingly telephoned Mrs Howard and explained that I should like to spend some time at the school talking with the staff: would that be acceptable? The poor lady could hardly, as a responsible citizen, refuse, but, to do her justice, she rose to the occasion by warmly accepting my proposal. She would even, she said, put a room at my disposal if I so wished. I did so wish, although quite

126

how I should best conduct the inquiry without disrupting the school unnecessarily, at the beginning of the academic year, I was unsure.

On Thursday 12 September, therefore, nearly five weeks after Adrian Carrick's death and two and a half weeks after we had been brought on to the case, Spooner and I moved into Grant College *en masse*, so to speak, to begin a concentrated inquiry into Carrick's professional life and colleagues. We began with the prefect of studies, a Mrs Tuesday Torrington, a spare lady with thin lips and a somewhat sour expression. Her study was on the first floor of the main building, squeezed in between a room devoted to gestetners and a store-cupboard (an arrangement that I am sure reflected no opprobrium on her status or performance). She listened in silence as I sketched in my belief that (1) Mr Carrick had been murdered (which she had heard already from the headmistress) and (2) the reason for his murder lay in his professional life. I then proceeded to ask her to comment on his standing with girls and parents.

'What makes for a teacher's standing, Inspector? Is it popularity? Is it getting the pupils through examinations? Is it a knowledge of the subject? Is it inspiring pupils to further learning – and how would you measure that? I put it to you, Gentlemen, that what gives a good teacher standing cannot be decided in advance, except for obvious essentials, and assessment is beset with so many imponderables, that I suspect there is no satisfactory answer. It's like asking How Hi is a Chinaman. So to ask me to comment on the late Mr Carrick's standing with pupils and parents is to skim the surface – to be superficial, in a word. Is that what you want?'

I was slightly nonplussed by this vigorous reply to what I thought was a simple question, but, preserving my courtesy as my mother had taught me at her knee, I said I was anxious to build up a general picture of Adrian Carrick in the hope of spotting some weak spot or hiatus wherein I could poke an accusatory finger: could she help in giving me a general picture?

'So it *is* a superficial view you want, Inspector. You could have made that plain at the beginning. Well, like all teachers – I venture to say – he was popular with some pupils, less so with others; popular with some parents, less so with others. This is all so obvious, Gentlemen, that I am almost embarrassed to mouth such truisms. Adrian knew his subjects, no doubt about that. The bulk of his examination pupils passed comfortably. His teaching style – and having sat in on some of his classes in a spirit of fraternal assessment, I can speak from experience – was lively and varied: good teaching practice, in short. Why might some pupils not have liked him? Why do some people prefer a tomato sauce on their pasta to a cream sauce? *De gustibus...*, Inspector. That I am aware of, there has never been any serious disciplinary incident, either here or at his previous schools, much less anything of a criminal nature. He attended staff and department meetings, met report deadlines, filled in the various administrative sheets that we circulate regularly, was always punctual for lessons, helped out with every show of willingness round the school. What else would you like to know?' she concluded abruptly.

Faced with such peremptoriness, I hesitated but continued undaunted. An inspector without intrepidity is not likely to advance his career.

'What happened to his wife?'

'She died of a heart attack. It was all over in a few days. A tragic business, but nothing to do with the school, of course.' No, it would not be, would it?

'How did Mr Carrick get on with other members of staff?'

'That's not an easy question to answer, Inspector.' She thought for a moment. 'I should say that he was more respected than liked. I do not in the least mean to imply by that that he was *dis*liked. No, not at all. The female staff had – how shall I put it? – affection for him but no real friendship. He was always very reserved, quite properly, in my opinion: in a mixed community like ours, where most members are female, a predatory male would be utterly undesirable, and I believe Adrian recognised that. He therefore kept his distance without being standoffish. Oh, dear, it's very difficult to express one's thoughts without seeming to do the man an injustice.'

'Were there any members of staff who were closer to him than others?'

'Well, possibly the head of physics, Mrs Costello, or the head of geography, Mrs Bryant: you'd be quite likely to see either of those two members of staff chatting to him in the staff-room, but it certainly never went a centimetre beyond that.'

'And was there particular friction with any member of staff?'

'No, I wouldn't say so. If he disliked anybody, he certainly never let it show.'

'Is it your impression that Adrian Carrick was happy here, both as a teacher in general and as a member of this staff in particular?'

Again Mrs Torrington hesitated. 'Yes, I should certainly say so,' she said slowly. 'You see, Inspector, the difficulty is that Adrian was so reserved, even shy, that he hardly ever spoke about himself. I don't think that even in the classroom he said very much about himself. Some staff, you know, use their own experiences a lot to get the girls' interest, but Adrian seemed to be keener to get the girls to express their *own* experiences in relation to whatever it was they were talking about. But yes, well, on the whole, if you press me, I should say that Adrian *seemed* perfectly content here. Now if there's nothing else, Inspector – '

Opining that this tight-lipped lady was unlikely to be of any further use and that I should prefer to converse with someone less acerbic, I said courteously,

'No, nothing else, thank you, Mrs Torrington, but perhaps you could ask the head of modern languages to meet us in the room set aside for us when he or she has a moment.'

We had not long to wait before a jolly, round woman darkened the door of our temporary interview-room.

'Daisy Craddock-Jones,' she said, with a hand outstretched as we leapt to our feet, 'head of modern languages. I understood you wanted to see me.'

'Yes, please, just a few minutes of your time, if you'd be so kind.' Having waited for her to be seated, I proceeded to offer the same introductory matter that Mrs Torrington had accepted so tartly, with the necessary adaptations to our new guest.

'Well, now, Inspector, let me first of all tell you something about the department. You'll want to hear that, I'm sure. You know, I often think it's a pity that languages are compulsory: pupils who don't take to French or Latin simply make teachers' lives a misery and learning difficult for the keener ones. On the other hand, I suppose if it weren't compulsory we might not have any pupils to teach at all! Anyway, the department consists of a German teacher, Mr Hubert Carraway, known universally, I regret to say, as 'Seed', the Spanish teacher who took poor Adrian's place, and two French teachers, namely, Mrs Quita Gardener and myself. We all teach another language when required. I hope all that is clear, Inspector.'

129

'Yes, perfectly, thank you. And now to Adrian Carrick?' I asked hopefully.

'Yes, of course, Inspector. Oh, and Sergeant too: mustn't forget you, Sergeant, must we? Adrian was a valued colleague. He was completely clued up in Spanish, making a point, for example, of spending at least two weeks a year in Spain imbibing current affairs and new expressions, visiting new places and so forth. Of course, for wider questions to do with how the department fits into the school, you'll have to ask someone else: I suggest Mrs Torrington.' I ignored this last suggestion.

'Did he fit well into the department?' I asked. 'Did he give himself airs, raise people's hackles?' I think I knew the answers to those questions very well, but I wished to hear them from the lady herself.

'Did he fit in? Yes, perfectly, Inspector. His manners were always exemplary, and his attitude to us was relaxed and fraternal without being in any way familiar. He contributed well to the discussions and always accepted either majority votes or my, um, rulings, shall we call them?'

'As far as the philosophy goes, who was his head of department?'

'Well, I suppose you could say he was. There was no head of philosophy officially – that is, in terms of salarial remuneration – but he was responsible for the subject in the Sixth Form.'

'Now please think very carefully, Mrs Craddock-Jones. I know you will have thought about Mr Carrick's death. Have you come up with any explanation for it?'

Before she could answer, however, there was a knock on the door, and Mrs Torrington's acidic head appeared round the doorway.

'Inspector,' the acidic head said, 'Mrs Howard thinks you ought to come straight away. We have just received some important news.'

I excused Spooner and myself from further talk with Mrs Craddock-Jones, expressing the hope that we should have the pleasure of a later conversation with her, when circumstances were more auspicious, and we followed Mrs Torrington along the corridor to the headmistress's office. Mrs Howard was looking upset.

'We've just had the most dreadful news, Inspector, and I thought you ought to hear about it straightaway. No details yet, but the main fact seems to be this. Young Claire Considine, who left us last year, has been stabbed to death in a shopping precinct in Cardiff.'

I must have looked slightly puzzled, because she added immediately, by way of explanation, 'Claire was a good friend of Geela Purdew's – if that's got anything to do with it, of course.'

'Ah!' I said. 'This is very sad news, very sad. Yet more tragedy. Thank you for telling me so promptly, Mrs Howard.'

In due course, naturally, the full story emerged, relayed by our Welsh colleagues. May I give you an account of it, in my own words? A visit to Cardiff enabled Spooner and me to visualise the sequence of events, although the police report was verbally complete: it relayed as much as was known at the time. Claire was the third child in a family of four, offspring of an accountant and his PR wife, who lived in Worcester. Claire had been uncertain which career path to follow, but in consultation with the careers staff at Grant, she had decided to try an honours degree in chemistry at the Cardiff School of Education, with a view to secondary teaching. (Teaching chemistry to spotty teenagers would not have been my choice, but it takes all sorts to make a varied world.) The University of Wales seeming to her to offer what she wanted, she applied and was given a place. She had travelled up to Cardiff a fortnight before she need have done, at the start of the academic year, not to take up residence but to acclimatise herself. She was determined to start as she intended to continue, steeped in the mysteries of the test-tube, Bunsen burner and pipette and agog to purvey her knowledge to eager(?) young minds. She was staying with a friend whom she had not seen for a long time, a former Grant pupil who had moved to Cardiff with her family when her father's job changed. The friend's name was Jocelyn. Claire and Jocelyn decided to walk from the School of Education Cyncoed campus to the Pentwyn Shopping Precinct, which was more or less on their way back to Jocelyn's house, so that Claire could buy a pair of shoes. The precinct was very busy. As they were weaving their way, in single file, through the other shoppers, Claire cried out, stumbled, fell and lay on the ground. A crowd quickly assembled. Jocelyn and a couple of men carried her to a bench, while someone else ran to telephone for an ambulance, even though it was clear to all that medical help was not what was needed. Pathological investigation established the cause of death as an injection of pure nicotine; Claire died in seconds, more or less painlessly. (Not quite a stabbing therefore, but near enough.)

I knew that I could, with every confidence, leave the investigation of Claire's murder to the local constabulary, but I felt I needed to be involved. I was convinced from the start that the murders of Claire Considine and Adrian Carrick must be connected. I reasoned as follows:

- Claire's death was not an indiscriminate killing, because no pathological killer would use such a method to strike down a random shopper: only someone who had followed Claire would know the opportune moment to strike

- only someone who knew Claire was going away from home for a few days would have followed her

- only someone with an interest in Claire and with intimate knowledge of her movements would have known she was going away from home

- only someone threatened by Claire in some way would go to the trouble of following her to Cardiff and murdering her as it were anonymously

- how could an eighteen-year-old schoolgirl be a threat if not in connection with the murder of another of Geela's circle of friends? It was too much of a coincidence otherwise.

Now I know that this line of reasoning was not foolproof, but it was sufficiently persuasive, I thought, to be put to the local investigating officer, a certain Detective Inspector Jonas Jenkins, an energetic, neat individual with a lugubrious face but a general appearance that was somehow reassuring; in his early forties; tall, eagle-eyed, crisply clean-shaven. If I was right, the clues to Claire's murder lay in Worcestershire, nearly seventy miles away, and Jenkins agreed, mournfully, that I should be free to conduct my own inquiries there, while he pursued what leads he could in Cardiff. Spooner and I returned post haste to Worcester, and our first call was on Claire's grieving parents.

The parents' income enabled them to occupy a comfortable and spacious house on the outskirts of Worcester. May I interject a political comment here, which is probably out of place but which I add as a private citizen, not as a member of the police force? My political persuasions are irrelevant to this case, as to all my cases, but some of socialist rhetoric seems to me to be saying, 'Pull the aristos down!' rather than, 'Pull the plebs up!', and I sometimes wonder what is wrong with the latter as a strategy! And I do not believe that thinking that makes me a fascist! However, back to the Considines. Mrs Veronica Considine was torn by grief, as well she might be, and made little contribution to the conversation. Mr Arnold Considine had mastered the outward manifestations of grief but spoke with restraint and difficulty. It was mid-evening by the time we had made the journey back from Cardiff, and daylight was fading. The lights in the sitting-room stared out at us as we approached the house, and we found assembled Mr and Mrs Considine and one of their other children, a lad of about twenty called Joseph. The atmosphere was understandably sombre. Fortunately a police constable had relayed the news to them earlier in the day, and that had given the family a short time to adjust to it. I was at least spared the terrible duty of conveying information about a brutal death in the family. I expressed, on behalf of the two of us, our sincerest condolences and briefly outlined my reasons for thinking that the leads we needed to follow were here in Worcestershire, probably at Grant, and that that is why local CID were on the case as well as their Welsh colleagues. I wished not to hustle the family unduly with questions, not at first anyway, but to give them time to speak and open their hearts if they wished.

'Inspector Wickfield,' Mr Considine said, 'it is completely beyond us why anyone should wish to kill our lovely Claire. She was clever, pretty, vivacious, with a whole useful future ahead of her. She never harmed anyone. It doesn't make any sense to us.' I turned to Joseph.

'Do you know anything, anything at all, that you think could shed light on your sister's murder?'

'Nothing, Sir. Claire and I were close. She would have told me about anything troubling her: danger, threats, problems, that sort of thing. No, when she went off to Cardiff for a few days, she was excited, carefree, perfectly cheerful as far as I could tell. She was looking forward to seeing Jocelyn and her parents again and to visiting the university as an enrolled student for the first time. The whole thing is inexplicable.'

I took a liking to Joseph: a frank, boyish face but the demeanour of a self-assured young man and a sort of gentle courtesy.

'I want you all, if you will be so good, to cast your minds back to the middle of the summer. You knew that one of Claire's teachers, Mr Adrian Carrick, died on Bredon Hill?'

'Of course, Inspector,' Mr Considine said. 'Claire attended the funeral. It was a major topic of conversation. Why should Mr Carrick have wished to kill himself? Upset over Geela didn't seem a sufficient cause, so we speculated endlessly on other possible motives for suicide. Such a very sad business.'

'Ah, well, you see,' I said, 'we have reason to believe that Mr Carrick was murdered.' There was a general movement of surprise at this intelligence, and I asked Spooner, with a nod of my head, to flesh out this bare statement. When he had finished, there was silence in the room, the only noise being a car in the street outside receiving a merciless revving up from an inept driver.

'Now, then,' I resumed, 'what if Claire knew something about this? The murderer of Mr Carrick would then wish to eliminate Claire as well.'

'But that's absurd, Sir,' said Joseph. 'What on earth could Claire know about it? Like us, like everybody else, she thought it was suicide. Nobody had ever mentioned murder to us.'

'That's what we have to find out,' I said. 'The murder of Adrian Carrick took place in the late morning of Saturday 10 August, nearly five weeks ago. Some planning had gone into it, certainly a few days' worth. The only thing we can uncover that might have any bearing on it at all is his last meeting with Geela Purdew on 6 August. Did you know they had met at a café in Pershore?'

'Oh, yes,' Joseph said. 'None of us attended the inquest, did we?' as he looked at his parents, 'but it was in all the papers afterwards. Claire was full of questions.'

'Right. Somewhere along the line Claire has seen or heard something and is known by the killer to have done so. It also seems probable to me that something has happened in the last few days to alert the killer that exposure was threatened. Now the inquest took place on 22 August, and the following day everything was made public in the press. The contents of Mr Carrick's last letter to Geela were disclosed, as were the topics of their final conversation. In fact, one could say that the whole business was thoroughly aired. So nothing there posed any threat to the murderer: it was knowledge available to anyone anywhere. My guess, therefore, is that Claire came by the knowledge that cost her her life either at school or more likely in conversation with somebody since the inquest. What I should like you to do for me, therefore, is to draw up a list of everyone Claire has been in touch with during the holidays, particularly in the last three weeks, but also before that, because we cannot afford to miss anything. I imagine that Claire's closest friends will attend her funeral, and Sergeant Spooner and I should like to take that opportunity to interview them – the ones from Grant, I mean - either singly or as a group. That should tackle the school end of the puzzle. When do you expect to hold the funeral, by the way?'

'We hadn't decided, Inspector,' Mr Considine answered. 'The undertaker is calling tomorrow to go over the arrangements with us. The whole thing is so unexpected we're in turmoil, but I should have thought in less than a week.'

'And where will it be held?'

'We have always attended St Stephen's in Barbourne,' Mr Considine continued. 'We shouldn't consider any other venue.'

'Would you be so kind,' I said, 'if it's not an intolerable imposition at this sad time, as to contact as many of Geela's and Claire's schoolfriends as you can and invite them to attend the funeral, explaining also that I should like an hour's conversation with them all afterwards? Would that be possible? And in the meantime, could I see some photographs of Claire, to try to fix her in my mind? Thank you.'

Fifteen

Claire Considine's funeral was one of the saddest affairs it has ever been my lot to attend. Her age, the circumstances of her death, the family's dignity and grief, the attendance of her school-friends, the ambiance, probably also the rich and heavy perfume of the white lilies on the altar, all combined to create a truly poignant and unforgettable occasion. The school had sent along a small selection of Sixth-Formers and some staff to represent Grant. The vicar, a diminutive, balding clergyman with a game leg, conducted the service with decorum and all due gravity, and I was impressed by his sincerity and by the fact that he seemed as genuinely moved as the congregation. Standing solemnly in the pulpit, he uttered the conventional sentiments of comfort from the Bible (but feelingly), with personal reminiscences of his own, and I was pleased that at the end of the service he allowed Joseph Considine to make a short tribute to his sister. I determined more firmly than ever to bring Claire's killer to justice.

The family had arranged for a reception at a hotel not far from the church, and those attending numbered, I thought, about seventy. I approached Geela.

'Hello, young woman,' I said, without, I hoped, excessive and unbecoming jollity in my greeting, 'I think Mr Considine mentioned that I should like a word with you and the other girls when it's convenient.'

'He did, Inspector.' She gave an enormous smile.

'How many are there of you?'

'Six,' she said.

'And who are they?'

'There's me, Denise and Iona, Jennifer, Kirsty and Nicola.'

'And when would be convenient?'

'That's up to you, Inspector.'

'Good, that's just as well, as I've fixed it all up already! Mrs Howard is kindly putting a room at our disposal – with tea and cakes later, would you believe? – and I've arranged for a minibus to take us to Grant immediately after this reception. We could have met at the station, I suppose, but the school will be a fitter trigger for all your reminiscences!'

I spent the rest of the reception, to which I and Spooner had been kindly invited, circulating as I could, but after half an hour or so I inquired of Geela, with a jerk of my head in the direction of the exit, whether we were all ready. Within a few minutes, the six girls, Spooner and I were bowling along to Grant College, a school for well-bred and monied young women. We negotiated the ornamental gates, drove sedately down the drive, noting the deer-park bathed in warm autumn sunshine on either side of us and the first signs of yellowing in the trees as we drew up in front of the school. It was a little after two in the afternoon, and, although we could see and hear some pupils engaged in games on one of the playing-fields, we deduced from the general air of peace that the bulk of the pupils were quietly seated at their desks imbibing Knowledge. Mrs Howard came down from her office to welcome us and had a few words with the girls, whom she welcomed back warmly despite the significance of the occasion. She took us to a medium-sized room, comfortably furnished, with windows giving on to the front of the school. A large table had been moved aside to allow the chairs to be set in a cosy circle, with a smaller table in the centre – to receive our tea and cakes, I surmised! Spooner and I sat apart from each other. It was on this occasion that I learnt the matter relayed to you at the start of this account of the case of Mr Carrick's death.

So that I could observe untrammelled, and so that Sergeant Spooner did not feel redundant, I invited him to open and conduct proceedings. I have had occasion before to remark to you that he was a presentable young family man, always neatly turned out, with a pleasant manner, usually tending to the taciturn but by no means inarticulate when times require something more – indeed, positively prolix on occasion - and with the ability to coax confidences out of his interviewees. There was no harm, and perhaps some benefit, in pushing him forward. He showed no sign of embarrassment, as a lesser man might, but plunged straight in with a pertinent few words.

'Girls,' he said, 'we'd like to thank you for agreeing to come along this afternoon, when there are probably plenty of other things you'd rather be doing – like sunbathing on the lawns or chatting to the present Upper-Sixth! No, no, seriously, we appreciate your time. Can we begin by introducing ourselves? You all know each other well, but remember that this is the first time the inspector and I have met most of you. Just say a few words each, please, to set the scene. Let's start with you, Geela.'

'OK. My name is Geela Purdew, I am an only child, I live in Pershore and I'm having a year out before going on to Exeter to read business studies with French.' She turned to her right.

'I'm Denise Phethean, I'm eighteen, my parents live in Aldershot because my father's in the army, and I'm at Reading, or will shortly be, reading geography.'

'I'm Jennifer Garforth, I live in Hereford, I have three older brothers who all bully me, and I'm reading English at Leeds.'

'My name is Nicola, Nicola Agnew, and I'm about to start at King's College, London, to do a degree in divinity.'

'I'm Kirsty Willibrod, my grandfather was German, and I'm about to start a modern languages degree at East Anglia.'

'My name is Iona, which means dove in Hebrew, because I'm so graceful and pretty to look at: Iona Micklem, all the way from sunny Aberdeen. I'm taking a year out to see the world.'

'Thank you all very much,' said Spooner. 'That imposing gentleman over there is Detective Inspector Wickfield, known to his lovely wife as Stan, while my name is Spooner, and that's all anyone ever calls me. Such a silly name, don't you think? Anyhow, I've got used to it after all these years. Now, let me just fill you in a bit on where we are. As you will remember, the coroner's inquest established suicide as the cause of Mr Carrick's death. We were then given information that another man was seen with him minutes before he fell to his death. This other gentleman, whom we shall call, let me think, Bubbles, told us that he had business with Mr Carrick; they had gone for a stroll together; and as they passed the head of the quarry, Mr Carrick felt faint and fell over the edge. Now Bubbles' testimony *could* be true – just – and we had to bear that point in mind, particularly as Geela remembered a comment of Mr Carrick's to the effect that he had suffered a couple of blackouts in the preceding months. However, in case it was murder that we were investigating, we followed other leads, looking at a possible Italian connection, for example, into which I needn't go as it led us nowhere, at Mr Carrick's private life, at his friendship with Geela, and at the beneficiaries of his estate. I admit to you freely that we were at something of an impasse –' he looked at me a little sheepishly – 'when the tragic news of Claire's death reached us. Now this *had* to tie in with Mr Carrick's death: we could not have two deaths, one of them doubtful and the other definitely murder, within a few weeks of each other in the same circle of acquaintances just by coincidence. In the light of this, it is now absolutely certain that Mr Carrick was murdered, and we shall catch up with our friend Bubbles in due course. He is known to be a hired killer, you understand: but we don't yet know who hired him; perhaps he doesn't either, and that could be a problem. It follows, however,' Spooner went on, 'that the most likely key to the two deaths lies somewhere in this room, amongst us.' He paused dramatically and looked round the circle of young faces. 'Now please don't jump to conclusions. I don't mean to suggest at all that one of you is responsible. Of course I don't. But one of you has the clue to the murders without knowing it. *That*'s what we need to uncover.'

As none of the girls spoke – probably a little intimidated by the strangeness and seriousness of the occasion and by the sergeant's solemn words – Spooner continued. 'What we hope to stimulate is memories. So I'm going to ask you just to talk: nothing else, just talk. What about? About your philosophy lessons, about what you remember of Mr Carrick, and about how Claire fitted into your circle. Do you think you can manage that?' Getting teenage girls to talk? And yet I detected no irony in Spooner's words! 'Someone start by telling us what she remembers of your very first philosophy lesson.'

There was a short silence until Iona spoke. 'Shall I begin?' she asked. 'Why not? Mr Carrick began the course with an overview of philosophy, and I still remember his definition of the subject: "the systematic attempt to understand the human world, with the aim of achieving a richer experience of life or, as we might say, 'wisdom'".

'How on earth do you remember that?' asked Kirsty.

'Because I'm clever, for one thing,' answered Iona, 'and for another, there's no point in spending two years on a subject without knowing what you're studying!'

Jennifer chipped in. 'He then gave us an overview of the various areas covered in traditional western philosophy: how we learn, how we decide what is right and wrong, how we relate to each other in a society -'

She paused to take a breath, and Denise waded in.

' – how to put a decent argument together, whether we can talk about anything that lies beyond our immediate sense experience -'

'the nature of language, whether there is a supreme being -'

'the nature of Mind -'

'*Et cetera*!' Nicola intoned triumphantly. 'No, honestly,' she added, 'there's a philosophy of history, a philosophy of music, a philosophy of science, a philosophy of religion, a philosophy of society: there's just no end to it, and we couldn't study all that, of course.'

'I see,' said Spooner, 'and what would you say are the highlights of the course for you?' He looked round the circle, aware that the mood was lightening and that the participants were loosening up.

'For me,' Denise said, 'I think it was Montaigne's scepticism and how Descartes took it even further, but only in order to refute it.'

'And does he refute it?' I asked.

'Philosophers are still arguing over it,' she said complacently. 'Mr Carrick's view was that Descartes had a good try but narrowly failed!'

'For me, on the other hand,' said Kirsty, 'it was the fallacies in logic. I simply loved the one called The Camel's Nose!'

'"The Camel's Nose"?' Spooner queried.

'Yes,' Kirsty explained, 'more properly called The Slippery Slope. You argue that because one thing happens – you ban pornography, for example – another thing is inevitable: in this case, that you end up banning all art which depicts the naked human form.'

'Yes, I liked that one too,' said Geela. 'It reminded me of the Lion and the Cheesegrater in *Lysistrata*: I still don't know what it means!'

Spooner looked across at Nicola. 'Oh, for me,' she said, 'it was Plato's argument about philosophers running the State. You remember that one, Geela?'

'I certainly do! Come on, what are we waiting for?'

The girls got up and struck poses at the edge of the circle of chairs. We all, naturally, turned to look at them.

'I'm Socrates,' Geela said, 'the clever one.'

'And I'm Glaucon, the simpleton,' said Nicola. 'Go on, you start, Geela.'

Geela: 'We can agree, I imagine, Glaucon, that a person who claims to be fond of knowledge can be believed only if he or she accepts to learn in every field. Otherwise he is only a dilettante.'

Nicola: 'Yes, I follow you so far, Socrates.'

Geela: 'In other words, a philosopher is one who pursues truth wherever it may lead. Now at this point we must distinguish three different mental attitudes: knowledge, which is of real things, ignorance, which is of what is unreal, and between them belief or opinion.'

Nicola: 'Yes, I follow that, Socrates. Go on.'

Geela: 'The object of opinion, therefore, can be said to fall between reality and non-reality: it is real but not fully real. Thus the person who appreciates beautiful things, for example, but fails to follow them through to what they point to – Beauty in itself – has grasped part of reality but closed himself to the fullness of reality. Only those who pursue reality to the bitter end, so to speak, are philosophers.'

Nicola: 'Yes, I accept that. It all seems perfectly clear.'

Geela: 'It follows, doesn't it, that the State should be in the hands of those who pursue final truth, not those who are distracted by mere *examples* of truth.'

Nicola: 'Yes, quite, Socrates, but how would you ensure that philosophers also have the other qualities needed to run the State?'

Geela: 'Well, My Friend, in my opinion, these other qualities necessarily follow from a dedicated search for knowledge. A person devoted to knowledge will not tolerate untruth; will not be diverted by incidentals; will exercise self-control; will not be grasping; will not fear death; will not stand for injustice; and as a consequence of all this, will be easy to get on with.'

Nicola: 'Yes, I suppose so.'

Geela: 'In addition, such a person will be refined and moderate, won't he?'

Nicola: 'Yes, I imagine he will.'

Geela: 'Then these are the people to whom we should entrust the State, because they combine all the qualities necessary.'

Geela and Nicola sat down to a ripple of appreciative applause. I must say that I was impressed that they could still remember this snatch of dialogue after what must amount to at least several months.

'Right, one more,' said Spooner. By this time, the girls were eager to talk, quite caught up in the exercise.

'I liked Aristotle best,' said Denise, 'and I'll tell you why. It showed Mr Carrick at his best.'

'How do you mean?' Spooner asked.

'Well, he didn't just explain Aristotle to us, as he did Descartes or Popper: he actually had something new to say which gave me the impression that I was part of history's understanding of Aristotle. Can I explain, Sergeant?'

'By all means,' Spooner said.

'Everybody up to now, Mr Carrick told us, seems to have understood Aristotle's *Ethics* to be talking about morality – you know, right and wrong, virtue and vice, that sort of thing. Mr Carrick showed us that that was a misunderstanding. Aristotle was talking not about right living as opposed to wrong living – virtue and vice in our sense - but about right living as opposed to failure: success as a human being, in short. Mr C took the example of a potted plant. Say your aunt gives you for your birthday a potted plant which you don't recognise, and she forgets to include the growing instructions: how are you to know whether it likes the light or shade, lots of water or a little water, a warm or a cool atmosphere? You can't know: you just have to go by trial and error, and it's unlucky for you if the plant dies while you're experimenting. Aristotle asked himself the question, What measures will ensure a successful human life? how can you make the most of yourself? Rather than let everybody try this or that out for themselves, he thought it would be a good idea to lay down some guidelines for those who were interested. So he identified, I don't know, a couple of dozen life-skills which you would need to practise if you were going to be a successful human being. Actually, if you count justice as one life-skill instead of a cluster, and friendship likewise, it adds up to twenty-three, I think, but it doesn't matter particularly. The life-skills are not virtues in our modern sense, as Aristotle's Greek is always translated. The book could perhaps be called *How Humans Flourish Best: A Guide to Successful Living.* It's completely misleading to view Aristotle as if he were trying to anticipate the Sermon on the Mount.'

'I see,' Spooner said. 'Very well put. Most enlightening; and the fact that you've remembered all that is certainly a tribute to Mr Carrick's skills as a teacher. Now I want someone to tell me how Claire fitted into the group. Iona, do you wish to start?'

'Hadn't we better start with Kirsty? She and Claire were best friends.'

'OK, let's start with Kirsty – if you don't mind, Kirsty.'

'Yes, but – ' she stumbled. 'If you want a full picture, you've got to go to someone who can pick out her faults as well as her – life-skills!'

'Oh, go on,' someone said. 'Just begin!'

'Right. I knew Claire from the start of secondary school. She was pretty lively, not afraid to make a fool of herself, keen to have a go at things she'd never tried before. Bright enough in class, but never top – in anything, I don't think! She was essentially law-abiding, even conventional, but occasionally she rebelled – quietly, so as not to rock the boat! She didn't go in for swear-words much, she didn't talk sex, she kept an eye on new girls to see that they were settling in, she was good but not excellent at sport, she worked pretty hard. What else do you want me to say?'

Spooner jumped in judiciously. 'No, that's fine, Kirsty,' he said. 'You've given us a good start. Now anyone else? Look, the girl's dead, we're hunting for her killer. Anything may be relevant. Just talk about her!'

'OK,' said Iona, 'I liked her, I liked her a lot, and like Kirsty I've known her since the beginning, but she could get on my nerves with petty whinges about silly little things.'

'I think she was quite religious.' This was Jennifer. 'Like most teenagers, she was a bit shy about admitting it, but I think she went to church with her parents – in the holidays, I mean – every Sunday. So she took life quite seriously.'

'She was quite a one for the boys: usually had at least one in tow,' said Denise. 'That's what being blonde does for you!'

'Yes, but I don't think she was into sex,' commented Kirsty. 'In fact, I'm sure she wasn't: she would have told me.'

'I don't think she read very much,' said Nicola. 'Newspapers, teenage magazines, that sort of thing, but not real books. I don't hold that against her; it's not a criticism: that's just the way she was.'

'She was always worrying about her hair,' Jennifer said again. 'She never seemed to get it right! Washed it every day, combed it, got highlights put in, cut it short, cut it long: never satisfied! But then that goes for many of us!'

'And she went on and on about her weight,' Denise chipped in, 'when she wasn't any fatter than the rest of us. Just a bit of puppy fat here and there, nothing to worry about If it wasn't her waist, it was her hips; and if it wasn't her hips, it was her boobs, or her bum, or her thighs. Dearie me!'

'How did she fit in with the rest of you?' Spooner inquired.

'Fine, quite one of the group!' Denise said.

I thought it was time I entered the conversation. 'Geela,' I said, 'you're very quiet. You haven't spoken for some time.'

'No, Inspector, I'm thinking.'

'A penny for them.'

'OK, what about this for a piece of logic?' Everybody else naturally fell silent. It was obvious that Geela was regarded as the leader of the group and that they respected her opinions. 'Let's go back to Mr Carrick for a minute. At our last meeting, and then later that day in his letter – one of the two letters read out in court – he expressed his inner turbulence – his "violent feelings", I think were his exact words. Now anyone wishing to do away with him could do worse than cash in on that mood of his. What I mean by that is, that a death which could be dressed up to look like suicide would be quite plausible in the circumstances: nobody would think of it as murder.'

'Yes, good so far,' I encouraged her.

'How many people knew we'd had tea together in the Abbey tea-rooms? or that he'd written to me? or that he was despondent?'

'Don't look at me,' said Denise, going slightly red.

'No, no, it's nothing to do with you, Denise,' said Geela. 'Let me finish! Mr Carrick asked me not to tell anyone, but I was so perturbed by the whole incident that I felt justified in discussing matters with Denise. She's utterly dependable and discreet.'

'Thank you,' Denise said *sotto voce*, clearly pacified.

'Now that's one thing Claire was *not*!'

'Who else agrees that Claire could be indiscreet?' I asked.

Quite a few hands went up, at half-mast, with index-finger outstretched.

'So what's your idea, Geela?'

'Claire got to hear something somewhere and blabbed, it's as simple as that, but heavens know what or where. You see, it's only an idea, and I haven't had time to think it through.'

'Right,' I said, 'the sergeant and I will work on that one.'

As if on cue, there was a knock on the door, and a trolley appeared with juice, tea and cakes for the assembled party. Our round table broke up, and we began to chat more generally, the purposeful tension of our talk dissipated in a hubbub of girlish voices exchanging news of the last two months.

On our way back to the station, with Spooner in the driving seat, my mind was grappling with the implications of what we had heard. I set out my thoughts aloud, partly to aid my own mental processes, partly to sound out my chauffeur, whose detection skills were second only to mine - ahem.

'We need to refine Geela's idea,' I began. 'I don't know about you, Sergeant, but I had also been working on the premise that Claire knew something about Carrick's death – presumably the identity of the murderer – and that this knowledge, in leaking out in a way we have yet to discover, threatened her own life. That may be accurate in its way, but it doesn't explain two things. Firstly, if Claire knew who Carrick's murderer was, why did she say nothing? Secondly, it doesn't explain, as Geela recognised, how someone got the information which suggested making his death look like suicide in the light of a self-accusing letter. So we need to go back a stage. Look at it this way – I apologise, Sergeant, if I'm being a little incoherent: it's known as thinking on the hoof, I believe. Let us suppose that what Claire leaks, probably without realising it, is that Carrick is depressed after his last meeting with Geela. That was Geela's suggestion. Claire tells someone who, unknown to Claire, rigs up the murder. Later on, Claire suddenly twigs that her indiscretion encouraged someone to commit murder. Now for Claire to be herself in danger, we need to suppose that the murderer has come to know that Claire can now identify the murderer, or at least indicate, presumably to the police, the path by which the murderer can be identified. We are looking for two leaks, therefore: one between the 6th and the 10th August and one more recently, in the days immediately preceding Claire's death: once the murderer knew of the threat of disclosure, he or she would have to, and would, act speedily to neutralise the threat. That is, the second leak occurred between the 7th or 8th of September and the 12th - probably.

'Now the first indication of Carrick's state of mind took place, inchoately, at the meeting in the teashop between him and Geela. The only person, apart from those two, of course, who knew anything about the contents of that meeting was, we are given to understand, Denise, and according to Geela, Denise is utterly reliable and discreet. So the leak was based, not on the conversation in the teashop, but on the letter. Who could have seen the letter? It must have been Claire! And whom could she have told? That narrows our window down to 8-9 September: Thursday afternoon to Friday, possibly evening, but probably morning, otherwise the plot wouldn't have had time to mobilise our friend, the unsavoury Johnnie Levers, before the Saturday morning. Our first question, therefore, which probably only Geela can answer, is: could Claire have read Carrick's letter between the 8th and the 9th September? Our second question, the answer to which we should get from the Considines, is: to whom did Claire speak 7-12 September. What do you think, Sergeant?'

'Brilliant, Sir!' but as he was concentrating on the driving, I am unsure whether he had taken in my subtle argumentation or how sincere he was in his estimation of it. I asked him to stop at the first public telephone box we came to.

'Geela,' I said, 'Stan Wickfield here. Could Claire have read the letter that Mr Carrick wrote to you the evening of your last meeting with him?'

'Let me think a minute, Inspector. Well, yes, I think she could have done. The day I got the letter, she was with Denise and me at my house. She came later, and Denise and I had already talked things over. However, I had left the letter open on my desk in my room. Claire went into my room for something – to get a tissue, I think – and she may have seen the letter. She wasn't gone long, but long enough to get a tissue and absorb the gist of the letter!'

'Thank you,' I said, 'that's all I wished to know!'

Sixteen

The following day, Friday, we had an interesting and, I thought, conclusive report from our doleful Welsh friend Detective Inspector Jonas Jenkins. It read (its tone will strike you as improbable in a police report in the latter half of the twentieth century, but I give it you as it came to us):

Death of Claire Considine, Pentwyn Shopping Centre, 11.05 am, 12 September 1974. My officers and I were determined to bring our investigation to a successful conclusion, despite the difficulties inevitably incumbent on an investigation of this sort. We were not in any way obstructed in our duties by intractable citizens or hampered by criminal elements – nothing of the sort: the reader will not imagine that the citizens of Cardiff would wish to impede us in any way. No, the difficulty lay elsewhere. Imagine the scene. It is a Thursday in September: warm sunshine, a populous city precinct, with the usual bustle of a suburb going about its business. There are no cars, but the place is full of people: the rich, the poor, the elderly, the young, mothers, grandparents, men, women: in short, a throng of ordinary citizens. One is busied with one's shopping, or hurrying to an appointment, or simply standing chatting with friends. Word goes out that there has been an accident. One takes steps to help, or moves towards the scene of the disturbance, or at least cranes one's neck to see. Then it is all over. Some hours or days afterwards, an importunate and irritating policeman invites one to identify suspicious, unusual or manifestly murderous people who had been in one's vicinity or in one's purview. The reader of this report will now appreciate our difficulty. People's memories failed to work. No one could tell us, Yes, there was this bloke, see, clearly not Welsh, or not a citizen of Cardiff, or with a five-foot scimitar in his hand, or with 'Hired Killer' tattooed on his forehead, and with my own eyes I saw him kill the poor lass. We advertised in the local press, we put up notices in shop windows, we spoke about it on local radio and television, and eventually we were satisfied that we had a pretty good idea of who had been in the precinct at the time of the killing: such is the helpful temperament of the Welsh. Then began the wearisome business of jogging people's memories. Yesterday we invited all those whose names we had gathered to meet us in the precinct, and we asked them to tell us where they had been standing, what they had been doing, who they had been with, what they had heard and seen. When I say 'all', I do not mean literally all: some made their excuses – illness, unexpected urgent business, a sudden attack of piles, that sort of thing – but we were satisfied we had a quorum. Lo and behold, out of this welter of sight and sound, of coming and going, of kaleidoscopic city life frozen at a moment, emerged a figure who, in our opinion, might be significant. We cobbled together this description: squat, say 5'6", broad-shouldered, heavily built, bandy about the legs; with the growth of a day or two on his cheeks and chin; heavy features, in particular a bulbous, red nose; close-cropped hair, bushy eyebrows; wearing blue jeans, blue shirt, black jumper or cardigan; aged about forty. There are two difficulties with this description, of which we at Cardiff are well aware. (I say this immediately to forestall any objection, however well-intentioned.) In the first place, it probably sounds as if we are ascribing a murderous action to a man purely on the basis of personal appearance. In the second place, the fact that he did not come forward to take part in our 're-enactment' is not proof of guilt: he could have been a stranger to the city whom our appeals to come forward did not reach. We do not see how we can provide a fully satisfactory answer to these difficulties, but we fall back on elimination: no one else in our trawl of the local citizenry emerges as a likelier contender. We hope very much that this account is of use to you.

The description of the gentleman singled out by DI Jenkins so fitted our friend Mr Levers that I had no hesitation in coming to two conclusions. One was that he and no other was indeed responsible for Claire's death, and I had no doubt that we should find some

Cardiffians willing to identify him. He would find it difficult to explain to an unprejudiced jury his presence in Cardiff at the moment of poor Claire's death. My second conclusion was that the principal who hired him for Claire's murder was the same as the person responsible for Carrick's murder. This was a very promising lead, as it gave us a handle with which to belabour Mr Levers.

Tomahawk was not, naturally, in residence at his usual lodgings when our uniform colleagues called that afternoon to have a word, but he was swiftly run to ground in the same part of London as before and brought to Worcester that same evening. I had the enormous pleasure(?) of another interview with my old friend. He had clearly not had time to wash either himself or his clothes in the recent past, but I overcame my distaste to the extent of conducting a proper and reasoned interview (I pride myself). We met in a cell at the station, where he looked less lively and more resigned than on our previous encounter. I hoped he realised that his previous position was now untenable, and that his best course therefore lay in cooperating with the police. I was within the 999th part of a spider's nose (to borrow a phrase of Edward Lear's) of putting a stop to Levers' career and of solving the two crimes which I was engaged in investigating. His heavy features creased into a slight smile of recognition as I entered the stuffy cell and sat down.

'Now then, Mr Levers, I think we have enough evidence to put you away for many years,' I said firmly and clearly but with my accustomed civility, 'and although I can't make you any promises as regards the court, it will do the families good if you come clean. The trouble is, you see, you are readily recognisable. You should have adopted a different career, My Friend, something a little less taxing, perhaps, like navvying or the merchant navy.'

Tomahawk said nothing but smiled wanly.

'So, out with it, then. First of all tell me what really happened with Mr Carrick.'

'I will, Inspector, I will. I've come to realise that spending my life dodging the police is no way for me. I've had enough. At least inside you're warm and fed. This is what happened, then.'

What follows is a bowdlerised and grammatically sanitised account, as before!

'I was minding my own business, as usual,' Levers said, 'and living my life quietly and wholesomely, when I got a note through my door: an envelope, it was, with a scribbled sheet and some cash inside. The note gave me three days to waste a bloke called Adrian Carrick, who lived at such an address and answered such and such a description. It didn't matter how the job was done, but it had to be made to look as if it could have been suicide: he had to fall under a train, or jump off a cliff, or shoot himself in the head. Half the money was given on account, the rest would appear on completion. You trust us, we'll trust you. It so happens I knew that part of the world pretty well, having been brought up not very far away, and I thought a little walk to a disused quarry, just to take the air, would do us both good. I prevailed on Carrick to accompany me by pretending to represent a firm of publishers with a proposition. I allayed his fears that I was an unlikely emissary of a publishing firm by assuring him that this was very unusual business for me, that I normally worked for a firm of vegetable wholesalers, that a friend, knowing I was in the district on business, asked me to drop in and sound him, Carrick, out. I told him I was walking over to St Catherine's farm near Bredon's Morton, would he care to accompany me for part of the way? He asked why I was leaving my car outside his door, and I answered that I sometimes got fed up with driving and felt the urge to stretch my legs. The walk to the farm and back would count as time off for my lunch-break. He also asked me why I was in a car and not a van, and I explained that the van was temporarily off the road, and I had been given a firm's car for a few days. He was a suspicious type, and I thought I would have to do the dirty in his own hall-way, but eventually he said he had thought of going for a walk anyway, and he was prepared to listen to what I had to say. It was his customary good manners (I surmised) wot undone him. We chatted about this and that, and I said the publishers, whom I named – I dreamt up a name, and he admitted he'd never heard of them - were interested in a factual account of teaching by a qualified and experienced teacher, with anecdotes of the classroom and staff-room, and comments on the state of the profession. When we had got up the hill to admire the view to the north, I told him my way lay on a track down through the woods by St Catherine's Well, round the grounds of Woollas Hall and so to the farm. I had a bit of a struggle to persuade him to come to the lip of the quarry, but he was not ready for what I had in store for him, and I overpowered him easily enough. As you can probably guess, Inspector, I'm no weakling. After that, I walked back to his house and drove off. A few days later another envelope was dropped through my door, and that was that – or so I thought. Then Danny Symons tipped me off that you'd been asking questions in the pub, and I ran for it until things should quieten down a bit. The thing is, you can't trust anyone these days. If they're caught by the police, they prefer to shop their friends than risk hefty sentences, and I was coming to the conclusion that I should settle down to a regular job. Honest, I was. Life would probably be a lot easier. And no, I have no idea who had contacted me. There was no signature, no post-mark, nothing but a scribble and a bunch of loose notes. I didn't care, anyway. And no, I haven't kept the note: what do you take me for? I'm not very clever, but I know evidence when I see it.'

'OK,' I said, 'now go on to Claire Considine.'

'This one was a little more difficult, because the girl wasn't in her own house but wandering round some Welsh town with a friend. As before, I got an anonymous envelope through the door, with a wad of cash – half my fee. There was also a photo, a name, and an address in Cardiff where this girl would be staying. I had, the note said, a three-day slot. So I tooled down to Cardiff, took up my post outside the address that I had been given, and kept watch. As you say, Inspector, my appearance is fairly conspicuous, so I did my best to smarten up and look as if I had business in the neighbourhood. On the second day, the two girls came out of the house, and I already knew which was which, of course. I followed them on the bus to the college, waited for them to come out, followed them again, this time on foot, to some shopping precinct, where I realised that conditions were favourable. I followed closely on their heels, and then, to my delight, the victim dropped behind as the pair tried to negotiate a cluster of shoppers. I was straight in there and straight out, walking away fast but without hurry as the cry went up. I was a long way away before anyone realised that the girl had not simply had an attack of angina. Another mission successfully accomplished, I told myself. To be fair to my employers, they recognised this too by handing in the rest of the cash a few days after my return to Worcester. However, when the whole business was splashed over the local press - here in Worcester, I mean - I felt a bit uncomfortable, so I hopped it down to London to stay with a friend for a bit. That's about it, Squire.'

151

The account was repugnant from every point of view, but I could not doubt that I now had the truth, or as close as to the truth as Levers was capable of getting. Levers was undoubtedly odious, but I am not called on to pass moral judgements on my fellows: only on their actions.

'Right,' I said, 'despite your denials, you must have some idea who employed you.'

'Straight up, Gov'nor, I've no idea. It's obviously the same bloke, as the envelopes and the writing were the same in both cases, but how can I say who pops an envelope through my door at dead of night?'

With that I had to be satisfied for the moment. What really peeved me was Levers' lack of remorse: he was cooperating because he was fed up with constantly evading the police, not because he regretted his horrible crimes. Anyhow, we had made progress, even though the crucial clue still eluded us. I arranged for a full statement to be made and signed by Levers before making my way to the Considines' house with Sergeant Spooner to see how the family had made out in listing Claire's contacts in the weeks preceding her death.

We arrived at the Considine residence in Worcester in mid-evening, to find the family assembled in the sitting-room. Mrs Considine was darning socks on a green wooden mushroom, Mr Considine was reading a newspaper and Joseph was watching television. At our entrance, the television was turned off, and the family prepared to sit down with us for a short discussion. Mr Considine spoke first.

'We've done what you said, Inspector. Asking round, we can find only four people Claire spoke to in the weeks leading up to her death. I don't mean only four people all told, of course. She said she wouldn't look for a job, not for a few weeks, anyway: she just wanted to be at home, lazing the time away, after what she claimed was a hard term. She saw quite a bit of Kirsty Willibrod, but she spent most of the time in the house or at the church, helping out with some new scheme the vicar has in mind. So apart from the family and Kirsty, Claire saw just four people to speak to at any length.'

'And who are they?' I asked.

'In the first place, there's her Uncle Douglas, who stayed five days in late August. Then there's a local lad called Landon Phillips, whom she's known since primary school. They've been mildly going out together, although I don't think there's much in it. There's old Mrs Pyle down the road, who's nearly ninety, housebound and almost blind and whose shopping Claire does several times a week. And then there's the vicar himself, Neil Shepherd. What precisely are you looking for, Inspector, if I may ask?'

'The sergeant and I,' I replied, 'have just come from a long session at Grant with Claire's old group of friends – which boils down to the bulk of the philosophy class run by Mr Carrick in the girls' last two years at the school. You probably know most of them, at least by hearsay. It was a very useful exercise and gave us much to think about. The thing is this, Mr Considine – and Mrs Considine and Joseph, of course – we now think that Claire saw a letter that Mr Carrick wrote to Geela Purdew. Perhaps I should say *the* letter: the longer one read out at the inquest into Mr Carrick's death. The coroner used it, you may remember, as part-argument for a state of mind bordering on the suicidal. Now if Claire told anyone else about the letter, it could have triggered a murder-plan in that other person's mind. Here was evidence that Mr Carrick was seriously disturbed, emotionally: in turmoil, to use his own phrase. What better moment to push him over the edge of a quarry and make his death look like suicide? Now that limits our investigation appreciably. Claire disclosed, maybe unknowingly, the first piece of crucial information to someone between Thursday morning 8th September and Friday morning 9th September. She then made a second revelation, again perhaps unwittingly, between Sunday 7th September and, at the latest, the morning of Wednesday 11th September. Whoever it was she told was either the murderer in person or a close acquaintance of the murderer. Now it is probably stretching our credulity somewhat to imagine that the murderer had two acquaintances in Claire's circle, so I think we're looking for the same recipient of both leakages, if I may so phrase it. Can you help us?'

'Give us a few minutes to put our heads together, Inspector,' Mr Considine said as he, his wife and their son Joseph went into a huddle over a sheet of notes, which I took to be their workings from a previous session.

'We're left with three of the four, because Uncle Douglas was not with us on the first occasion. So that leaves Landon, Mrs Pyle and the vicar.'

Having obtained the addresses of these three people, Spooner and I took our leave.

'Now, Young Sergeant,' I said in avuncular fashion as we returned to our car, 'do you see things the same way that I see them?'

'And what way's that, Sir?'

'Of these three, the vicar, being a man of God, is above suspicion. We may surely say the same of Mrs Pyle, a housebound old lady heading for her last decade of the century. That leaves young Landon Phillips. He's the one, you mark my words. So,' I continued, without giving Spooner a chance to comment, 'let's start with him.'

Seventeen

Although it was getting late in the evening, we thought we could risk a call on Landon without getting him out of bed. We accordingly knocked on the door of No.6, Lea Close, a few hundred yards to the west of the Considines', and to our gratification a young man answered the door to our summons.

'May we come in?' Spooner asked courteously. 'We're CID officers investigating the death of Claire Considine.'

Landon was a lanky youth with a curl of yellow hair over his forehead, trousers supported well below his hips and bare feet, but he had an open, pleasant face.

'Come in,' he said without any awkwardness, leading us into the front room. 'Mum and Dad are out, but can I be of any help?'

'Yes, it's you we've come to see!' Spooner said.

'Me? But I don't know anything about Claire's death!'

'Well, no, you may think you don't, but perhaps you do without knowing it.'

'I'm not sure I follow you, Officer,' he said, appealing to me.

'Look, Landon,' I said, 'can we sit down? Then we can explain things.' When we were settled and I had tied in Claire's murder with Carrick's, I resumed the conversation.

'This is how it is. We're looking at two dates: the 8-9 September – that was a Thursday and a Friday – and 8-11 September, Sunday to Wednesday. On the first occasion, Claire told someone, perhaps you, that she knew something about Carrick's state of mind before he fell to his death in the quarry. On the second occasion, she spoke about it again but in such a way as to hint that she knew or guessed who the murderer was. Now, does any of that ring any bells?'

'"Bells?"', he said. 'Yes, it does, actually. Funny you should mention bells, Officer. It reminds me of a conversation Claire and I had at about the time you mention – shortly before Mr Carrick's death. She came round here with what she called a little piece of gossip, which I took little notice of at the time but which came back to me when the papers reported his suicide. She said she had just discovered that her philosophy teacher had fallen for one of the class and made a bit of an ass of himself: wasn't that hilarious? Well, to be honest, I wasn't very interested, as I didn't know Mr Carrick.'

'And where do bells come into it?' I asked.

'Claire commented that the affair sounded like an adaptation of *Doctor Pascal* without the spontaneous combustion! I then said, "Pascal? That rings a bell!" and at that very second the phone rang. Yes, a curious coincidence.'

'I see. Now, did you tell anyone else about what Claire told you?'

'No, Inspector, it wasn't of sufficient interest to me. Why should I go round blabbing about someone I'd never met?'

'And what about our second slot: 8-11 September?'

'Um, let me think. No, wait a minute, that was last week, wasn't it? I didn't see Claire at all, or anyone else if it comes to that. The firm I work for sent me off for a week's course in Stourbridge. I left on the Sunday afternoon and didn't get back until the Friday night, and it was then that I heard Claire had been killed in Cardiff. It came as a shock, I can tell you. I can still hardly believe it.'

Spooner and I came away little the wiser, and, moreover, wondering whether Claire had not been too young to be reading Zola. Ah, the youth of today!

'What do you think, Sergeant?' I asked.

'Nice enough young fellow,' he commented. 'I believed him when he said he hadn't spread the gossip, but in that case, our conversation with him hasn't got us very far, has it? What about you, Sir?'

'Mm, same here. We'll call it a day, since we can hardly visit either of our next people at this time of night. See you in the morning!'

At what I took to be a seasonable hour, we called on Mrs Pyle the following morning. Her terraced house was neat and clean, with vases of cut flowers here and there. She tottered to the door to answer our knock and preceded us, still tottering, to the sitting-room, where she flopped gratefully into an easy chair. She showed her age in her features, but mentally she was alert, even lively, and she was clearly glad of someone to talk to.

'Officers,' she said, 'I hope you'll stay for a cup of tea. I don't get many visitors, you know, not at my age. All my friends have gone, my husband died years ago, and my children are away, and it's a very sad age to be living to, don't you agree? All on my own, stuck here in this little house with only myself for company – well, there's the carer, of course, she's a great help, and Claire. Poor Claire, how I miss her!'

'Yes, it's about Claire that we've come, Mrs Pyle.'

'Oh, is it? There's nothing anybody can do now, you know: dead and buried, poor lass. She was a great help to me.'

'Tell us, Mrs Pyle, did she ever mention to you a teacher at her school called Mr Carrick?'

'No, I don't recall the name.'

'Did she ever talk about a teacher who was attracted to one of her fellow-Sixth-Formers?'

'Oh, yes, *him*, you mean? Was that his name? Yes, she told me: she thought it would amuse me, I suppose. Didn't he commit suicide over it?'

'Well, not exactly, but can you remember whether you told anyone else about it?'

'What, me? Who else would I tell here? Joan, the carer? Of what interest could it be to her? I ask you! No, Inspector, I don't spread gossip. I much prefer to talk about the old times. Joan often gets me to take out my photograph albums, and she listens while I ramble on about this person or that, or this or that holiday that Bill and I had, or what the children got up to when they were young: you know the sort of thing. So I sit in my chair here, going over old times, reminiscing, gently mouldering away until, I suppose, one morning I shall wake up dead, and it will all be over.' She sighed.

We took our leave, without partaking of tea, confident that the carer, who had just arrived, would take over where we left off.

'No,' I commented, 'I can't see anything very much leaking out of that house. Gossip might go in, but I doubt it would ever go out again. But Claire certainly seems not have minded very much what she told to whom. We're not getting very far, are we?' I added despondently. 'There's only the vicar left, and I have no very high hopes of him.'

The Rev Canon Neil Shepherd occupied, naturally enough, the vicarage next door to the church. He was in and received us amiably. Spooner explained our business, and he ushered us into his study, where books lined the walls and a general air of learning reigned. He composed himself to speak, with his lame leg outstretched.

'A very sad business, Gentlemen, very sad. One of my liveliest young parishioners: so helpful, so willing. Such a loss to us! You know, I sometimes wonder what the Almighty is about, allowing such things, but that has been the cry of us ignorant men from the very beginning, and I know no one who has yet come up with a satisfactory answer – not even the sages of Israel. We are poor creatures, Gentlemen, wrapped up in our sins and bounded on all sides by inadequacy and imperfection. Yes, it's a dark world we inhabit, but we cast our cares on the Lord! I'm sure you agree.'

'Yes, indeed, Canon – very affectingly put, if I may say so. Now to come to the point of our visit. Did Claire at any time mention to you that she knew about the unrequited love of a schoolteacher for a Sixth-Form leaver at Grant College for Girls? Actually, I've phrased it poorly, but you probably know what I mean.'

'Ah, I think I can guess the case you're referring to, Inspector. You mean the sad business over – what was his name's? – death: you know, the man who committed suicide by jumping into a quarry.'

'That's the one,' I said, 'only it wasn't suicide. So what's the answer to my question, Canon?'

'Did Claire tell me anything about it? She told me she knew both the people involved, of course – she naturally would, wouldn't she? – but by then it was in all the papers anyway. We did discuss the case, as it had upset her very much. She told me she had the highest regard for Mr Carrick, and what surprised and disheartened her most was that such a devout man should consider taking his own life, rather than abandoning himself to the divine mercy. She was also saddened by the media coverage: the papers rattling it around, with a view not to the human drama or to Mr Carrick's reputation as a sincere and honest man of the highest integrity, but to their sales' figures. I comforted her as best I could, assuring her that we are all in God's hands and that God would take the poor man's soul to Himself. We talked quite freely together about it, and I hope that my poor words were of some consolation to her: we can speak only as the Spirit inspires us, and yet the inspiration is poured into poor vessels at best.'

'You mean that you and she talked about it only *after* the media reports of Mr Carrick's death?'

'Yes, of course, Inspector: what could she know about it *before* his death?'

The conversation meandered on for a bit, but we gained nothing more from our visit to the Reverend Canon. To say I was deflated is an understatement. We had achieved virtually nothing, and we were no closer to solving Claire Considine's murder – until, that is, I went home, despondent and baffled, to have a spot of lunch with my wife.

My wife Beth is a woman of outstanding qualities, not the least of which is the ability to tolerate my vagaries and idiosyncrasies over so many years. Since I have related elsewhere how we met and married[7], suffice it to tell you here that she has been of incomparable assistance in more than one of my cases, generally, I suppose I must add, unwittingly! As we sat at table, chewing on pork sausages, she discerned – wonderful woman! – that I was preoccupied.

'Come on, Stan,' she said, 'out with it! You're miserable company at the best of times, but today you're worse than ever, and I don't see why I should put up with it. What's it all about?'

After swallowing my present mouthful, I gave her an account of our recent efforts on the case and added that I could not see my way forward: my options were running out.

'You could always look up Uncle Douglas, you know,' she said. 'You seem to me to have dismissed him much too lightly. Even though he couldn't have received Claire's early confidences, he could later have picked up information – say that Claire had rumbled the identity of the murderer – and passed it on, unknowingly, of course. But I've got a better idea. You see, Stan, your trouble is that you lack imagination.'

'Imagination?' I said, aghast. 'Me, no imagination? Who told the boys all those stories when they were young? Not you: it was always my job, for some odd reason.'

'Take it from me, Stan, you're a plodder: earthbound and prosaic. If you don't know yourself any better than that by this time, it's a pretty poor show, I say.'

---

[7] *The Will of Joan Goode 1793*, chapter XVI (JF).

'OK,' I said, 'what have I missed now?'

'Go back to your interview with young Landon Whatever-his-name-was: Phillips. He told you the phone rang while he and Claire were talking about Carrick's affection for Geela.' When she paused, I said, somewhat lamely,

'Yes, he did. It rang bells. Zola and all that.'

'Well, can you imagine the scene? The phone goes. Landon answers it because he's sitting on top of it in the living-room. "It's for you, Mum!" he shouts. He lays the receiver down on the table, or some other surface nearby, and the two youngsters continue talking, oblivious of the person on the other end of the line. That's how their conversation was overheard. After a while, Mrs Phillips picks up the phone in the hall, and Landon replaces the receiver his end. Now admit, you didn't think of that, did you?'

'It's a bit far-fetched,' I objected.

'Maybe,' she said, 'but had you even thought of it?'

I admitted bitterly that I had not: how ignominious to have to capitulate to a woman!

On my return to the station, I immediately telephoned the Phillipses, but there was no reply. I should have to bide my time until the evening. In the meantime, I discussed my latest brain-wave (shh: mum's the word) with Spooner.

'Well, Sir,' he said, 'I think that's a quite brilliant idea. It deserves a medal. How *do* you do it?'

'Brains, Spooner, that's all there is to it: brains. Some of us have them, some of us don't. You probably make up for them in other ways, and one day we may find out how.'

'Thank you, Sir, for that modicum of confidence. In the meantime, I feel as if we're on the verge of a solution.'

'So do I, but my question to you, as we sit here twiddling our thumbs in this frustrating interval, is: who for heaven's sake are our suspects? We don't seem to have any! I can't think of anybody who meets the case, not a single soul.'

'*Nil desperandum*, Sir: we're possibly about to find out, but I can point a finger at a few people.'

'Oh, yes: who?'

'Here's a few suggestions. Maurice Carrick.'

'Why?'

'Because Adrian has rumbled Maurice's international art swindle carried on from his Birmingham gallery.'

'Next!'

'Mrs Phyllida Cruickshank?'

'Why?'

'Because she saw Carrick having tea with Geela and couldn't bear the ignominy.'

'Next!'

'Colin Purdew.'

'I know: because he thought Carrick was seducing his daughter. Rubbish! Go on.'

'Winslow Carrick.'

'For what possible motive?'

'Because of a childhood grudge.'

'Next!'

'Mrs Joyce Barlow.'

'Don't tell me: because he rebuffed her and she couldn't stand the shame. Anyone else?'

'Yes, Mrs Howard.'

'Mrs Howard? That's absurd! Why?'

'Because she was afraid that Carrick's behaviour would bring the school into disrepute.'

'Crikey, young fellah me lad, you've got an extremely lively imagination: I think you ought to get it seen to. Look, Sergeant, this is all quite ridiculous. We've been over every possible motive. You could mention everyone with whom we've come in contact during this case and concoct some motive - even, I daresay, for good Mrs Pyle. In fact, the vicar of St Stephen's is surely our prime suspect: a man with a game leg and a bald pate – his guilt stands out a mile. No, no, we shall just have to sit this out in patience. I tell you what: why don't we retire to separate corners and do some serious thinking for once?'

'For once, Sir? That's an insult!'

'Yes, well, never mind that now. I shall see you later, Sergeant, and I hope I shall find you on the ball.'

When we reconvened, my face must have been wreathed in smiles, because Spooner looked at me sharply and asked what the matter was.

'Matter, Sergeant? While you've been spinning gossamer webs of speculation and fantasy, or even dozing quietly in the canteen, I've been solving the case! I went over all my notes again, carefully, and I know now who the murderer is and the motive for the crime.'

Gratifyingly, Spooner's jaw dropped.

'Get away, Sir! So who is it?'

'Funnily enough, it's somebody whose name we don't know and whom we have never met: after all these interviews and whizzing round the continent! And to prove to you that I'm right, I'm going to make two predictions: when we telephone the Considines in a minute, we shall find a) that whoever it was that phoned while Claire and Landon were having their conversation lives in Evesham and b) that Claire visited Grant during the first week of term.

Spooner duly picked up the telephone and dialled through to the Considine residence in the city. It was answered by Mrs Considine. I could not hear her replies, but Spooner put her the two questions the answers to which we needed to know, and when he came off the phone, he was smiling.

'Well, Sir,' he said, 'I don't know how you do it, but the call in question was from a Mrs Chloe Walsh, and she lives at number 117, Albert Road, on the outskirts of Evesham!'

'It follows, Sergeant, that our murderer lives at number 115 or number 119, Albert Road. And did Claire visit the school during the first week of term?'

'Yes, on the Thursday!'

'Told you so. Right, let's be going.'

I was pleased to be at the end of the case, but I reproached myself for the amount of time and effort we had wasted in the course of the inquiry. It was now Friday the 20th of September, virtually six weeks

162

since Adrian Carrick had met his death. If I had had my wits about me – if I had not made the unforgivable mistake of failing to test the evidence – we could have made an arrest on 2nd September, six days from the start of our inquiry, and so saved Claire's life. Have you ever read Publius the Syrian? He was a freed slave in the century before the birth of Christ, who left behind a collection of pithy sayings. One of these sayings reads, 'While we stop to think, we often miss our opportunity'. Well, I missed my opportunity because I did *not* stop to think. (Another of Publius' maxims might better meet the case: 'Nothing can be done both hastily and prudently'. I leave these maxims with you.)   I have the guilt of Claire's death on my conscience. (By the way, Courteous Reader, do you ever tire of my *obiter dicta*?   I try to keep them to a minimum, but my mental processes are extremely lively and will not be stifled! In any case, my wife tells me that they are, all things considered, one of my most endearing traits, although in the present instance, of course, my *obiter dictum* is a particularly melancholy reflection.)

Spooner drew up outside number 117, Albert Road. For those of you who do not know it, Albert Road, Evesham, is a long (and busy) street which juts out aggressively from the High Street towards the west, then turns south, backing on to market gardens and open countryside and forming the western limit of the town. The southern end of this north-south leg consists of rows of terraces of four houses each, while the northern end, after a break to allow Blind Lane and Avon Street to intersect, consists largely of detached houses. It was to one of these that Spooner drove. Having checked that Mrs Walsh was (with her husband) the owner-occupier of number 117, Spooner and I, according to Mrs Walsh's instructions, knocked on the door of number 119. It was answered by a woman in her fifties, dressed for the house but stylishly. I could see at once, even before we had introduced ourselves and shown the badges of our authority, that she was apprehensive: more than that, she knew that we were her nemesis. Without a word, she turned slowly on her heel and slunk into the front room, where her husband sat reading a newspaper in front of the television. Spooner gave the usual caution – to both husband and wife: they must, by my reckoning, have been in the plot together.

'Do you wish to tell me how it all came about,' I asked, 'or shall I tell you?'

'I'll tell you, Inspector,' she said. 'It's a relief, in a way, to be found out. I probably look to you like a hardened criminal, beyond the reach of remorse, but I'm not. Carrick I didn't mind so much, but Claire - !' She put her hands to her face and sobbed. 'It all started when Larry here got into trouble at work and went down for a year. I thought he'd learnt, but he hadn't, and the same thing happened again. Rather than be found out, we decided to disappear and start life afresh elsewhere under a new name. His first disgrace had been in all the papers, and I wasn't going to have fingers for ever pointed accusingly in my direction, so we moved here and I immediately began looking for a job: not easy in early August! I'd been looking at local schools and phoning round but having no luck: of course not, so late in the day. One morning, Chloe from next door was round here having a cup of tea, when she let drop that there was a bit of scandal to do with a teacher at Grant and that she wouldn't be surprised if he was dismissed for it or, more likely, topped himself rather than face the shame. I know now that she hadn't quite interpreted the data fairly, but I was getting desperate by this stage, since we were running out of money. A couple of discreet questions in a pub put me on to a certain person who wouldn't ask any questions, and that was the end of Adrian Carrick. I stepped nimbly into his shoes, on the basis of a couple of well-crafted testimonials: professionally inexcusable, resorting to forged credentials, but I couldn't help myself.

'Even before term started, I had moved myself in to his old classroom, got my head round my new post and was beginning to think everything had settled down. The coroner's court brought in a verdict of suicide, and that was the last I heard. Then in the first week of term Claire Considine wandered into the classroom one break, on the pretext of asking whether there might not be a set of Mr Carrick's philosophy notes she could have, as she'd lost hers. We got to chatting about Carrick, and she happened to mention that in her view his death wasn't suicide: quite out of character, she said. She was going to do a bit of sleuthing on her own, she went on, looking for people who might have benefited from his death. She was all rather vague – and terribly amateur, of course – but if ever she went to the police with even the whisper of a suspicion, I'd be done for. She had to go, or Larry and I would never find peace. That's it, in a nutshell, Inspector. In confessing to you, I have now found peace of sorts.'

It gave me some satisfaction, after my inexcusable blunder, to explain to Spooner how I had come to the conclusion that the key to Carrick's murder lay at Grant College.

'At the back of my mind niggled a piece of information that I knew rang false. When I revisited my case-notes in depth this afternoon, I remembered what it was: Mrs Howard, the headmistress, hired a new teacher to replace Carrick on the strength of two written testimonials. She explained her reasons for doing so: shortage of time before the start of the new academic year, improbability of employing anyone but a probationer if she advertised, pressure of events at a time when girls and parents were seeking advice over the newly-released examination results – and I accepted these; but it occurred to me to wonder why an experienced teacher should be proffering testimonials instead of names and addresses of referees, in particular her last employers. Her actions began to appear fishy. I then thought that if she had come to hear of a teacher of her own subjects who was in, let us say, suicidal mood, the next step would suggest itself.'

'That's very good, Sir!'

'Child's play, really, Sergeant, but I was in such a hurry to get our investigation moving, that I didn't properly test each step of the way. I can't take any credit for our success, I'm afraid.'

'And how were you able to predict that our bird lived at number 119, Albert Road?'

'I reasoned that somebody new to the area – and I didn't see why that part of the story shouldn't be true – would get to know next-door neighbours first of all; that's all.'

'Wonderful!'

Thinking it would be a courtesy to inform Geela of the results of our day's labours, I gave her a ring in her French *château*. I imagined the dazzling, turreted mansion on the edge of a lake, in the depths of a silent forest, the only denizens of which were the boar and the deer out for their evening grazing ... After a short delay, the flunkey who answered the telephone put me through to her – a little grudgingly, I thought, but that is neither here nor there.

'Geela,' I said, 'Stan Wickfield here. I hope you're not too busy for a quick word.'

'Inspector, my day's labours are at an end. I was amusing myself

165

sitting at my window, gazing out over the moat to the forest beyond: such a peaceful scene. So no, you're not disturbing me. In any case, it's always a pleasure to hear you.'

'Ooh, you flatterer!' I said. 'I just wanted to tell you that the case is now concluded,' and I proceeded to give her a summary of our findings and of how Claire' indiscretion had led to her death. I could imagine Geela on the other end of the line digesting all this information.

'How do you feel about things now?' I asked solicitously. 'It's all over. Mr Carrick's reputation for integrity and existential truth – is that Karl Jaspers, or am I coining a phrase? – is intact. He has been laid to rest.'

'Yes, he has, thanks to you, Inspector,' she said slowly and then added, after a slight pause, 'It's a pity he's not here to receive my forgiveness.'